All the Men We

LOVE

A Novel

Jamillah A. McDaniel

A story of first generation college graduates and
their journey to become complete women

Emitym Books
P.O. Box 115330
Atlanta, GA 30310

Manufactured in the United States of America

10   9   8   7   6   5   4   3   2   1

Library of Congress Cataloging-In-Publication Data
Title: All the men we love.

Copyright Registration Number: TXu001091003 /
Date: 2003-02-14

Copyright Claimant: Jamillah A. McDaniel

Revision Date: 2012-4-30

I. Contemporary Fiction

ISBN-13: 978-0615636092 (Emitym Books)
ISBN-10: 0615636098

.

dedication

Taurus N. Nelson, Jr.
May 6, 1991 - January 17, 2010

To a young man that showed me the true meaning of unconditional love. I will always love you Taurus. May you live and rest in peace.
Love Auntie

acknowledgements

My first acknowledgement is to the Father, God, my creator for bestowing the gift of storytelling on me and stirring it to completion. I thank my mom, dad, sister, and brothers for supporting me throughout the production of this book and in life. I also want to thank my friends and extended family, my aunties, uncles, cousins, nieces, nephews, grandparents, great aunts and uncles for all their love and support.

A special thanks to my sister, Akilah, who helped me produce the paperback copies of this book and who is my best friend in the whole world. Thanks to my friends from Clark Atlanta University who always support my endeavors, Roxanne for her invaluable insight during the editing process, and Kim Harris and Painting It Red for hooking up my cover artwork.

Finally, I want to thank everyone who encouraged me growing up in that small community known as Sobrante Park in Oakland, CA and everyone who purchases a copy of the book. You truly inspire me. I love you all.

Chapter 1 graduate school shuffle

Cameron rushed out of the apartment to catch the 7:45 morning bus on her way to school. She trotted down the two-lane road towards the bus stop. The cold wind gusted against her face, whipped her cheeks and caused her lips to dry and tighten. Almost out of breath, she panted and watched the morning mist heave from her mouth as she waited for the traffic to die down. Her opportunity to make a break for the bus stop would come soon. Standing at the corner of the block, Cameron could see the illuminated sign of the bus approaching her: 77 SOUTHERN STATE UNIVERSITY. Cameron took courses at Southern State University to complete her last year in the school's Master of Business Administration program. She had to make the bus on time to attend the lecture prior to the final exam.

She ran across the road, praying the driver of the Volkswagen Bug would slow enough to allow her to make it. The blowing horn abbreviated her stride. Cameron's heart rate accelerated while she dodged the oncoming traffic. She continued to run. The bus stopped at her feet and she faintly smiled, exasperated, as the bus driver opened the doors.

"You know I would've waited for you," Mr. Sam replied. Cameron always felt that Mr. Sam, the usual driver on her route, was like an uncle. He greeted her every morning with a brilliant smile. When he gave a boisterous laugh, his stomach would bounce against the large steering wheel.

"I know," she paused to catch her breath, "but sometimes you're not driving."

"Well when I am, you don't have to worry."

Cameron smiled between pants as she grabbed hold of the rails for balance up the three high steps of the bus, "Thanks; I'll keep that in mind."

Cameron observed the handful of people on the bus route before taking a seat near the back door. Most people in her neighborhood did not commute using the public transportation system. In fact, the bus usually did not fill until it reached Chestier Bridge Road, more than two miles down the street. In the Atlanta area, it was common to leave an affluent neighborhood and be minutes away from a lower income community.

The clutch in her Honda Civic had given out a month ago, and she could not wait to drive her own car again. Her roommate's cousin leisurely worked on her car while allowing her time to come up with the four hundred dollars she needed for the repairs. He understood her financial situation. She was a fulltime student with a part time retail job at a party supply store. Usually, he would finish a job in a day and charge a storage fee if a vehicle was left longer than three days. Cameron appreciated the favor because he already reduced her cost by charging her close to nothing for the labor.

When Cameron graduated from high school, she moved to Atlanta from Oakland to attend Brownsberry College, a small but reputable historically black college for women. Cameron could not get used to the seasonal weather changes, especially cold winter days like today. The weather had hit a wind chill factor of ten degrees this particular morning. Cameron still missed the beaches and marinas she often visited when she needed peace of mind in her birth state. Today, she needed water. Although, she had to admit, the greenery of the trees had a similar tranquility as the ocean waters.

Cameron pulled her newly acquired Bible from her backpack and read a scripture for encouragement. She joined a local church after searching for three years. Her gift from the church was her Bible. *Trust in the Lord with all thy heart and lean not to thine own understanding, Proverbs 3:5.*The scripture had become one of her staples as she found herself a college graduate with no job prospects. After acquiring her degree, the doors of opportunity did not swing off the hinges as everyone around her expected. Instead, Cameron fell into the ranks of other college graduates with a degree in accounting and a lackluster career trajectory. She enrolled in Southern State University's Master in Business Administration program after completing her undergraduate degree in accounting. She hoped she would have more career opportunities after completing a master's degree. Lately, Cameron felt helpless because she had a part time job, no savings, no car, and to top it all off, she still lived a single life.

Cameron tasted bitterness in her mouth, and felt a film on her tongue. There had been no time for breakfast this morning. Placing her tongue on the pallet of her mouth, she swallowed, feeling the grit from her tongue again. She recognized the taste of morning breath. She had forgotten to brush her teeth in her rush to get to the financial management class on time.

Cameron looked out the bus window and admired the high priced homes she hoped to purchase one day. The neighborhood that she lived in was very peaceful, a big change from her Oakland community where gunshots and loud music competed for the higher decibel range. The angst of being one semester away from a graduate degree made Cameron nervous and filled with pride simultaneously. No one in her family completed college. In addition to being the first to graduate from college, she would be the first one in her family to achieve a master's level education. She often downplayed the accomplishment around others. In her opinion, she had no choice. Besides, she knew plenty of first generation graduates. Two of her closest friends in Atlanta were the first to graduate in their own families. Tomiko, her fearless college roommate, and LaShaun, who majored in accounting with her and currently, shared an apartment with her.

Cameron awoke from her daze and rung the bell to notify Mr. Sam he was approaching her stop. She grabbed her backpack, hurriedly placed her Bible in it and flung it over her shoulders.

"Thank you," Cameron yelled from the back of the bus.

The bus driver waved her on, "I'll see you tomorrow sweetheart."

The bus stopped directly in front of the building where her Financial Management course took place. Cameron walked up the stairs leading to the building of her classroom. The all brick building sat somewhat off the street and the double glass doors were below the gold raised letters on the building, MANOR HALL.

As soon as Cameron entered the building, the smell of fresh roasted coffee fumigated her nostrils. A handful of students, who were not in Cameron's class, gathered in a makeshift cafe with three small tables and two chairs at each table positioned to the right of the door entrance. Cameron's class doors were to the left. If she had five extra minutes, she could purchase a mocha latte. She walked into the classroom with a minute to spare.

Mr. Jameson, a tall and confident man, walked down the stairs of the classroom to take his place in the front of the room. Mr. Jameson's receding hairline distinguished him and most of the other professors in her school. He began lecturing while every student feverishly took notes, with the exception of those few students half–asleep – like her classmate Tony.

Cameron described Tony as "culturally ambiguous" because he claimed a Native-Mexican-African-American heritage. Today, Tony reminded her more of a lazy American.

After fifty minutes of continuous lecturing, Mr. Jameson turned from the white board, placed the cap on the dry erase marker, and pulled out a handkerchief to wipe the beads of sweat from his forehead. The curly red hair covered his head like two massive cotton balls plastered to both sides. He rolled up the sleeves on his blue and white gingham-checkered shirt and placed his hands on his waist, "Are there any questions?"

Silence fell across the classroom. Each student humbly evading the professor's stare, in a silent plea to end the class rather than brave a question possibly leading them into another fifteen minutes of lecture. The professor looked up at the discouraged faces in the auditorium style seating and continued, "This test, like all others this year, will not be graded on a curve. So my advice to all of you…" He paused and scanned the lecture hall of over one hundred students, "is to study hard."

The sounds of loud sighs and books closing waved across the classroom. Tony jerked up, wiped the drool from the sides of his mouth, and rubbed his brown-skinned face to ensure he left no signs of sleep behind. He looked around to see if anyone had noticed him.

Cameron shook her head in disappointment and teased, "It must be nice to sleep through class. I guess you got it like that."

"Cameron, give me a break. You know I work late nights at the club." Tony stood from his seat and crossed the aisle. "Excuse me." He paused in front of her, "Can you get me a copy of the notes?"

Cameron laughed, "I'll see what I can do Tony."

"Thanks Pookie. I'll call you later." Tony kissed Cameron on her forehead. Cameron and Tony studied together when she first started at Southern State University. A few months into school, Tony started working as a party promoter for an Atlanta nightclub. His schoolwork suffered as the late nights took all of his energy. When he actually made it to class, he ended up falling asleep partway through it. Since then, they rarely studied together and he took on a more brotherly role in Cameron's life. She sensed he was in school because his father slated him to work for the family business, a company that produced cleaning products located in Southern California. She felt Tony was lucky to have a guaranteed job after graduation.

The thought of working a mediocre job just to pay rent unnerved her. Being a new graduate in the aftermath of the attacks on the World Trade Center in New York City was unsettling too. As the economy continued to plummet, businesses tanked from the unsteady market. She enjoyed Business School or 'B School' as the students called it at Southern State, but she started nurturing her desire to become an artist by reciting poetry at local venues in Atlanta a few months earlier.

After Tony left, Josh leaned on the edge of his seat towards the row in front of him where Cameron sat packing her backpack. He tapped Cameron on her shoulder, mimicking Tony and teasing her. "You got all that *Pookie*?"

"If you got the gin and tonic," Cameron replied sarcastically.

Josh was the total opposite of Cameron. In some ways, Cameron envied him. He already had a job interview with Merchants, an international consulting firm and he never had to fret over his skin color or gender being a hindrance to him advancing in his career. Josh laughed in the boyish way that made Cameron want to laugh too. "Come on, it's not that bad. You always ace the tests."

Cameron half turned in her seat to look up at Josh, hoping not to give him a whiff of her morning breath. "Are you kidding me?"

Josh stood six-feet tall and had an athletic build. Before his knee injury, he played cornerback for the North Carolina Rams, a semi-professional team. Josh raised his eyebrows, "What did you get on the last test?"

"I got a B plus."

"I rest my case." Josh continued packing his bag, methodically placing his notebook, pencils, and breath mints in the proper sections of his over the shoulder backpack.

"You don't have a case to rest," Cameron continued to argue. "A B plus and an A are two totally different grades."

"That's pretty damn good though for this class. Do you know how many people are failing?"

Cameron pointed her index finger at Josh. "Don't do that! That's the same thing Mr. Jameson said when I tried to get him to reconsider the grade for my last assignment."

He shook his head back and forth. "Cameron, please don't start that again."

"No, I think that he really feels like *I* should be satisfied with making a B plus at *this* school. I know I'm an A student." Cameron began feeling more and more like her career pursuit was leading her down a road to a jobless future. Power-hungry men dominated the field that she would be entering and Cameron did not fit the description, at all.

"It's not because you're black," Josh said. Cameron and Josh had held this debate many times before, but no one could convince Cameron otherwise.

"Well, fortunately for you, you're not black or a woman, so you don't have that concern." Cameron huffed and turned back towards her desk. She knew that Josh believed she would not be here if she did not have the ability to make the grade. Other classmates did not feel the same way about the African-American presence at Southern State. Some assumed that affirmative action quotas helped Cameron — and students like her — gain admission into the school's prestigious program based on race and not academic merit. She felt as if African-Americans received a green light after all the other racecars had already lapped them four hundred times, and then expected to catch up.

"I'm gone, Cameron. I gotta get ready for the interview with Merchants this afternoon." Josh stood, pulled the strap of his bag on his shoulder, and looked toward his classmate and closest friend in Atlanta. He did not understand her frustration but he was sympathetic to her and he wanted her to stay encouraged. He evaded the conversation with her about race and gender in America. "Study group at my house this weekend?"

"Sure." Cameron turned around to avoid seeming emotional about her friend's imminent departure. His job interview reminded her of how much closer he was to finishing his degree. She knew the position with Merchants meant more to him than graduating itself.

"Good luck on the interview." Cameron feigned support and insincerely muttered. She had her own selfish reasons for not wanting to see Josh leave town for a job. He was the first person to approach her during orientation week at Southern State. Meeting a friendly face during orientation made the transition from a historically black college to a traditional school less grueling. At Brownsberry, she was not just a number. The professors took the time to reach out to her and it was nothing like her experience at Southern State.

"Thanks Cam! I'll see you this weekend."

Cameron rose with her backpack strapped to one of her shoulders. She walked a few steps behind him fiddling with the zipper on the smaller part of her bag to pull out her cell phone.

Cameron felt the hurried steps of someone behind her and stepped to the side to see Meagan approaching her. She stopped short of trampling over Cameron.

"Hey girl, what's up?" She asked Cameron in a pitchy voice.

The voice irked Cameron. She felt Meagan was an opportunist – a trait that would be good in a future career, but did not help when building relationships with her peers. Meagan and Cameron were in the same strategic planning course last semester. The teacher divided the class into small groups, and Cameron ended up with Meagan and three other girls. Meagan did not start acknowledging Cameron in the group until the day after she saw her and Josh having lunch in one of the student cafeterias and she continued to talk to her after the course ended because she was Josh's close friend.

"Meagan, what do you want?" Cameron asked grudgingly.

"Nothing, I just want to know what you have planned for the weekend."

"Studying, studying, and more studying," Cameron answered while walking out the classroom and fumbling through her cell phone menu to retrieve her missed call log. "The only thing that is going to be on my mind this weekend is this final."

"I thought I heard Josh mention something about a study group. Is there room for one more?" Meagan crossed in front of Cameron to cut her off and gain her undivided attention. "I have a copy of the test." Meagan offered Cameron with a yearning for acceptance in her dubious hazel eyes, "You're more than welcome to get a copy of it; *if* you want it."

"How do you have the test?" Cameron was already suspicious of Meagan's motives.

Meagan dismissed Cameron's accusatory undertone, "Some second year students from last year gave it to someone that I know."

"What do you want from me?" Cameron knew anything Meagan gave away had a price.

"Nothing," Meagan rolled her eyes and combed her fingers through her shoulder length blonde hair. "Jeez Cameron, why are you so defensive all the time?"

Cameron did not reply. She stood firm, placed her hands across her chest, and waited for Meagan to respond to her with some integrity.

"Okay, okay-I know that you and Josh are studying this weekend, and I..." Meagan quickly continued, "I just want to be invited to the study group; that's all."

Cameron laughed, "Are you serious?"

"Yes and what's so funny about that?" Meagan looked at Cameron with a concentrated stare, failing to find the humor in her statement. "Cameron, you gotta help me out. I promise you won't regret it. He won't even look in my direction some days. I don't understand what's up with him."

"Wow. That's amazing." Cameron paused for a minute, and looked at her phone again. "It's been almost two years, and you still have no clue." Cameron took a moment to entertain the thought of Meagan joining their study group for nothing more than Cameron's amusement. "We haven't discussed any details, but I'll give you a call once we confirm the times."

"You are my girl for life." Meagan raised her hand to Cameron for a high-five.

Cameron raised her palm in the air but stopped short of giving Meagan a high five. "Save it, Meagan."

Cameron's cell phone screen indicated she had three messages. She played them back: "This is Tomiko. I know you are in class half sleep, so wake up! About tonight…give me a call because something might have come up in the last day or two…okay in the last hour or two, but give me a call. Love ya'." She expected Tomiko to call. They had a standing date at Starbucks before the poetry event tonight. Cameron deleted the message and continued to listen to the remaining messages.

"It's LaShaun. Call me when you get a chance." Delete.

"What up Cameron? I just wanted to know if you were trying to get on the list tonight. Holla at ya' boy." Delete.

Cameron returned her phone calls in order of importance. First, she called Yusef, the last voice mail message but the most important. Yusef almost never answered his phone. He would listen to his messages, and if he felt it was important enough, he would call back.

"Yusef, definitely get me on the list tonight; remember the poem I told you I was working on, Venus Fly Trap? I finished it and I'm ready to recite it."

Yusef hosted the most talked about open mic poetry event in the Atlanta area. He leased the spot in downtown Atlanta, the Poetry Lounge.

Next, she called her roommate, "What's up?"

"Where have you been?" LaShaun's tone was almost motherly.

"Class. *What's up?*"

"When are you leaving campus?"

"LaShaun, I don't have time for twenty-one questions. Let me know what you need. You know these are my peak minutes." Cameron had no patience for people calling on her peak minutes, especially when the conversation entailed giving accounts of her whereabouts. She had a tight budget, and paying overage minutes was not what she wanted to do with any extra money she came across.

"You're awfully crabby today." LaShaun made the sound of a cat hissing. LaShaun always made that sound when she thought someone acted bitchy. "I just wanted to know what time you are leaving the house tonight, because I may ride out with you-I mean, you know, I'll drive tonight."

"That should be fine. I need to talk to Tomiko just to be sure, because we may not meet at Starbucks. If that's the case, I'll be leaving a little after eight."

"Okay, call me back."

Finally, Cameron called Tomiko, the last on Cameron's callback list because it took more effort to deal with her sometimes. Tomiko had a "the world is mine" attitude that Cameron admired and appalled at the same time.

Tomiko answered the phone as if Cameron were a business client, "Hello, Tomiko Bordeaux"

"Hey Meeko. It's Cameron. What's up with tonight?"

Tomiko dropped her professional business mode. "I'm not going to meet up with you at Starbucks tonight. Michael came by and he's taking me out to dinner. I guess this is him trying to make up with me."

"Why do you do this song and dance with Michael? He is too good of a guy for you."

"Oh, I don't deserve a good man?" Tomiko retorted. "Girl, you can save that for a talk show, because I ain't tryna' hear it. I'll talk to you soon."

"I guess we'll have to hook up another day."

"Oh, I'll be at the Poetry Lounge. I'll just be getting there a little later than usual. Michael's taking me to Justine's, and I don't pass up a date to Justine's."

"You don't pass up a meal."

"Don't play with me Cameron and save me a seat tonight."

"No problem. You should bring Michael with you. He would probably have a good time."

"Please, and you should bring Corey." Tomiko hung up the phone before Cameron could respond. She felt exposed at the mention of Corey's name. His name was taboo for anyone in her inner circle, and had been for six months since Cameron last spoke to him. Cameron didn't have time to deal with Tomiko right now. She had two more classes to attend, and then she could begin her day as a poet. Right after she brushed her teeth.

Chapter 2 the vow of celibacy

Tomiko counted down the seconds until five o'clock. Although it was unusual for her to leave the office that early, she promised to meet Michael for dinner. On a normal day, her eight to five turned into a seven to nine. She never regretted the late nights she spent on the job to ensure projects received the attention they garnered. Her success depended on her exceeding any expectations her employers had of her. As a young business executive at a prestigious marketing firm, she already earned the trust of her superiors. Her new client, Urban Gear, was a chance meeting during a social event she and Michael attended for one of his many influential social groups. When she pitched the opportunity to her immediate supervisor and managing partner at the firm, Henry Wallace, he gave her the go ahead to develop a proposal. She credited it as her chance to show the owners and partners of Wallace and Baker she possessed the wherewithal to manage a client from conception to close.

Tomiko unlocked her file cabinet and grabbed

her black Coach handbag from the drawer. She sat in her executive style leather seat, pulled out a palm size make-up compact and applied foundation to her smooth fair skin. She looked at her naturally curly hair in the mirror of her compact and ran her fingers through to loosen up the curls. Michael would be shocked when he saw her new hairstyle. Tomiko felt a sense of control when she excited Michael's emotions. Any man that wanted her would have to cater to her. Unfortunately, Michael was her sacrificial lamb. At twenty-six, she realized she had a destructive pattern in relationships. After the climax, she no longer wanted to be bothered with the man.

When Michael initially called her earlier in the day, she declined his invitation to go out. Michael was not accustomed to rejection and Tomiko was well aware of his status in the single's market as one of the most eligible bachelor in town. At Michael's persistence, she finally accepted his invitation on the condition they meet at six and leave at eight.

Her office phone rang a minute after five, right before she could finish applying her lipstick. A phone call after normal business hours usually meant a client had a problem, and they know they can reach her at anytime, or it was a personal phone call. Either way, her devotion to her job and those she loved were a priority. She had to answer it.

"This is Tomiko," she answered the phone with the lipstick tube in her hand.

"What up, bitch?" A loud female voice hollered into the phone.

"*Charlotte?*" Charlotte was the only person whoever called Tomiko a bitch and got away with it.

After graduating from college, she and Charlotte only spoke to each other when she was in town for a business trip or on vacation. She was sure that her mom must have given Charlotte her work number, and that did not bother her. She missed talking to Charlotte on a more regular basis.

"Yeah, it's me. I know you didn't forget about ya' girl." Charlotte and Tomiko had grown up together in Chicago. They were best friends from kindergarten through high school.

"Now you know I haven't forgotten about you. What are you up to and how is my lil' man?" Charlotte's son, Devin Junior, was Tomiko's godson. Tomiko thought that he deserved a better name because, as far as she was concerned, his father's life was nothing to emulate.

"Lil' Dee is cool and his dad is still on my nerve; but I love the both of them."

"Let me call you on my cell phone; I was just heading out of the office…"

Charlotte interjected, "No boss lady, I wasn't calling to keep you long. I heard you're gonna be in town next week and I just wanted to holla at you."

"Yes, I'll be out there in a week. You want me to call you when I get in town? We can hook up for lunch or something."

"That sounds good. I'll talk to you then."

Tomiko hung up the phone feeling a sense of disconnection between her and Charlotte. The conversation did not seem as natural as it did when they were younger. She never understood how the two of them used to be so close and now they seemed so far apart.

Tomiko snapped out of her reminiscent trance and finished applying her lipstick. She smacked her lips together, evening out the application, and walked towards her office door.

"Tomiko," Henry Wallace greeted her belly first, with a grin that added rouge to his plump cheeks. "How's my all-star player?"

"I'm doing great Henry." Tomiko hurried to pass her boss, mentor, and co-founder of the firm Wallace and

Baker.

"Leaving so soon?"

"Yeah, I have to get out of here, but I will see you early tomorrow morning." She continued to walk with the hope her short answers discouraged him from engaging her any further. Nevertheless, her hurried pace did not stop him from his press of questions.

"It must be something really important," Henry continued fishing for information. "I don't remember the last time I've seen you leave the office before seven."

Dedicating her life to the office had become the expectation, not the exception. She smiled and politely dismissed herself, "I'll see you later Henry."

Tomiko pressed the button to call the elevator. She felt Henry behind her, ready to ask his next question. "How are the negotiations going with Urban Gear?"

She turned toward Henry, whom she felt would not leave her alone until he had a promise of some sort of work update from her. "I should have it on your desk tomorrow. Hopefully my trip next week will be a closing, and the beginning of a new relationship with them." The doors of the elevator opened and Tomiko stepped in, expecting him to come along with her.

"That's what I like to hear." Henry swung his forearm across his midsection indicating to her that she did a great job. A wave of relief hit her and she relaxed her shoulders when she realized he would not be riding the elevator with her. She did not want to talk about work anymore. She had her mind fixated on the curry chicken, plantains, rice, and peas she would be ordering from Justine's.

"I'll see you in the morning." Henry waved and walked off as the doors were closing.

The elevator opened to a security booth encased by glass windows. Franklin, her favorite security guard, sat in the booth watching his show on a black and white television set with rabbit ear antennas and a dial that turned the channels. Franklin was old school to a fault and a father figure to her. The two of them had held many short but meaningful conversations in this parking garage. If her father were in her life, she hoped he would have been like Franklin. She tried to buy him a remote control color television monitor last Christmas, but he would not accept it from her.

"Hello young lady! I'm glad to see you are getting out of here early today." Franklin raised his navy blue baseball style cap with a gold security emblem from his head as a salutation to Tomiko. Mr. Franklin's curly salt and pepper hair was cut short but full on his head. He was a former service man, tall, slender and physically healthy for a man his age. Although Tomiko never asked, Mr. Franklin was no more than sixty years old.

"Thanks Mr. Franklin," Tomiko paused to chat with him. "It does feel good to leave early today."

"You're too young and beautiful to waste your time in here all day. You gotta get out there so that you can live a little. Believe me, I've been here twen-tee-five years," he scolded, enunciating twenty-five with assurance, "and this building and these companies are going to be here long after you gone. I promise."

"I know Mr. Franklin." She appreciated his concern, but times were different now. His generation made it possible for employers like Wallace and Baker to hire them. Her generation had something else to prove. Even with equal rights and opportunities, the responsibility to succeed bore down on her shoulders like the will of her ancestors to survive. If they could survive the physical abuse, she could definitely handle the intellectual hazing.

"Well, be safe young lady. I'll see you tomorrow."

"God willing," Tomiko replied.

Tomiko approached her luxury Lexus sedan, opened the door, threw her purse in her passenger seat and pulled out her parking stall. She eased her car into the traffic on Auburn Avenue, a historic street not too far from Martin Luther King Junior's birth home and the King Memorial Center.

Tomiko made a left out of the parking deck and headed towards Peachtree Street. Cars lined the street for blocks. She slowly cruised by high rise office buildings owned by banks, downtown shopping centers, the Hard Rock Café, what was once known as Planet Hollywood, the Hilton, and nameless other buildings. Once Tomiko passed the shadows of the skyscrapers, she made her way through Buckhead, a ritzy part of Atlanta, located just miles from the infamous Lenox mall. On any given day, you could spot local celebrities leaving or going into the mall. Justine's was located in the heart of Buckhead. During her early college years, nothing could keep her from its active nightlife. Tomiko still visited the area to dine at some of the restaurants during happy hour and to entertain clients.

She pulled into the parking lot at Justine's. Maurice, the valet, approached her. He was a young familiar face at the restaurant and dressed in the customary valet uniform-a red vest, white button up, black bow tie, and black slacks. "Hi Tomiko," he held the door open as she grabbed her handbag and made her way out of the car, "It's always a pleasure to see you."

"It's good to see you too Maurice," Tomiko appreciated the valet's good customer service and always tipped well. "Make sure you park me close."

"Yes ma'am." He handed Tomiko a ticket and parked her car along the border of the bank and Justine's parking lot.

Tomiko approached the host standing behind the station as she studied the seating chart placed underneath a small lamp on top of the podium.

"Hi, I'm here for Michael Alexander." Tomiko interrupted the woman.

"Yes, Ms. Bordeaux, we're expecting you." The host moved to the side of the podium and grabbed two menus. She led Tomiko to a table for two and set the menus down, but Michael was nowhere in sight. "Your waiter will be with you in a moment."

Michael was known for his work in architectural engineering. He designed the floor plan for Justine's; its wooden floors, open bar and spacious dining areas created a cozy treasure in the Atlanta dining community. Celebrities frequented the spot because the restaurateur had produced hit songs for most of them.

"Is he here?" Tomiko asked impatiently.

"Who, the waiter?" The host smiled awkwardly and attempted to avoid answering too many questions from Tomiko.

"No is *he* here? *Michael?*" Tomiko placed her menu down and her elbow on the table and folded her hands together. She did not appreciate the woman playing dumbfounded with her.

"Oh, Mr. Alexander will be here momentarily," she started to walk away but Tomiko stopped her with a demanding and authoritative tone.

"No, I asked if he was here, not when he would be getting here." Tomiko persisted, agitated with the quick and vague response, "because if he's not, I'm not waiting for him."

The unsuspecting girl did not know how to respond to Tomiko's aggression towards her. Her job had been to seat Tomiko and keep her at bay until Michael arrived. Before she could come up with a response for Tomiko, Michael showed up.

"I'll handle this," Michael tapped the host on her arm and reassured her that she handled the situation okay by slipping her a generous tip.

"Where are you coming from?" She started at Michael, "You know that I don't like waiting."

"Tomiko, I just went to the bathroom." Michael looked back and pointed towards the restrooms. "I watched you harass the poor hostess for a minute before I stepped in to save the poor girl."

"Well, you should have saved her since you set her up like that and if you were in the bathroom, why weren't the menus already at the table?"

"Because they don't seat you until your party is here."

Tomiko looked at Michael with an uneasy stare, "That's a bunch of bullshit. You know she would've sat you at a table whether I was here or not. You're just getting here, aren't you?"

"So shoot me Tomiko. Look did we come here to argue or make up?" Michael grinned.

"I don't have anything to make up for," she reminded Michael.

Michael sat back and ran a hand over his goatee on his dark face, "You are a trip."

The waiter interrupted them, "Good evening ma'am," he nodded at Tomiko, pausing as she greeted him with a faint but pleasant smile. "Sir, today's special is a mango grilled tilapia with black beans, coconut rice and fried cabbage. We have a sweet potato dumpling as our soup of the day. Can I get you any beverages to start out with this evening?"

"I need something strong," she stared at Michael with disdain, leaned back in her chair and crossed her arms.

Michael chuckled at Tomiko's antics. Sometimes she acted as if she cared for him and about their relationship. Michael stopped trying to figure it out. He knew what he wanted and he planned to show her exactly what she needed.

"Ma'am," the waiter continued, would you like our drink menu?"

"No, I'm good," she leaned forward and waved

the waiter off, "a water for now, lemon on the side please."

"Very well, and for you sir?"

"I'll take a dirty martini."

"A dirty martini for a dirty ol' man." Tomiko laughed.

"I got your dirty ol' man. I see this dirty ol' man has you smiling again."

"Michael, I don't want to play games with you. I'm here to eat and get to stepping. Don't think I've forgotten either."

"Tomiko, look I am sorry. I got off work late and I was dead tired when I got home; that's the only reason I didn't call you. I've tried to call you for the past four days and…" Michael paused and looked at Tomiko, bringing to her attention he noticed her long hair was gone and replaced with short fine curls. "Why did you cut your hair?"

"It was time for a change," she replied nonchalantly.

"Yeah, but babe your hair was beautiful."

"Is that the only thing you thought was attractive about me, my *hair*?"

"I mean, it just fit you. You know I loved when you wore your hair down and now it's just…" Michael paused before he made a remark that would send her flying out the restaurant in a rage. "Never mind," Michael replied to prevent an outburst from Tomiko. "The cut looks good on you."

"Thank you." Michael's compliment did not seem sincere but the more it raised his eyebrows, the more it satisfied her. Something about the whole situation gave her a sense of control.

It was a quarter to eight when they finished dinner. Michael pulled Tomiko's seat from the table and she grabbed his hand as he led her out the restaurant.

Tomiko waited a short time for the valet to drive

her car around, but it was long enough for Michael to strike up a final conversation with her before they departed for the evening. "What are you doing with the rest of your night?"

"I told you, I have plans this evening, but I will talk to you later." Tomiko kissed him on his cheek. "Thanks for dinner."

"I understand you have plans this evening but what about later tonight? Are you going to come by my place?"

Tomiko walked towards Michael and said in a low voice, "Michael, I'm not having sex."

"*What?*" Michael asked in a voice a pitch higher than normal. "I didn't ask you about sex. I just asked if you were coming by tonight."

"I'll talk to you later." Tomiko waved and smiled as she stood by her car door while the valet hopped out.

"Wait, Tomiko. You can't be serious." Michael pleaded with her.

"Oh, but I am." She tipped the valet as he held the door open for her and drove off toward the Poetry Lounge. Her cell phone rang. The screen read that it was Michael. She did not answer.

Tomiko identified her issue with intimate relationships and she was ready to deal with it spiritually. For some reason, she lacked the will power to say no to sex. If she wanted it, she had it. It took a Sunday morning sermon from her Pastor for Tomiko to begin to understand the self-destructive patterns she nurtured back in her teenage years. She preferred men who were non-committal and relationships of convenience. She would have to turn her weakness to God if it would be resolved. Her vow of celibacy was something she had been contemplating for over a year. She knew it was something she had to do for herself, and Michael would understand eventually."

Chapter 3 venus fly trap

"I can't see you anymore
 Because every time I do,
 A little piece of me
Goes with a little piece of you.
Every time my phone rings
I pray it's your voice on the other line
But it's only my girl asking
'What are we doing tonight?'
I know we said we'd keep our distance
 So neither one of us gets hurt
But I know you see
How not being with you is killing me.
So, I can't see you anymore
Because every time you're going, "uhm-uhm"
 And I'm going "ooh-ooh"
 I keep thinking in the back of my mind
This has got to be more than just sex to you.
And if it's not,

Why do I keep treating you like my king?
Day dreamin' and fienin'
On how you make me cream
And waitin'…for another shot at what?
'Cause I know this has to be everything you want.
When I'm away from you
It takes the strength of ten thousand men
To keep me from callin',
And while you hide behind
The feeling of lust
In love I've fallin'.
I've fallin' and I can't get up
So it's going to take more than one of those
Push button monitor phones
To bring me back around.
I was so high on cloud six-nine,
I didn't know I left the ground.
But wait…
Let me get back to the point
Of why I can no longer see you…
I'm ready to give you everything,
My room, my womb, my keys, my heart, my soul,
The secret to my daddy's gumbo.
Damn boy, this ain't no mumbo jumbo,
And that's why I can't see you anymore,
So call me when you're ready for love."

The crowd greeted Cameron with applause, most of them standing to their feet as Cameron finished reciting her poem. Yusef came up to the stage to take his place as emcee and gave her a hug as she exited to take her seat.

"Give it up for Cameron the Chameleon, cause she be changin' the game on ya'll. I told ya'll the show was going to be hot tonight." Yusef echoed on the microphone.

"You ain't no virgin." Tomiko blurted out as Cameron approached the table. Secretly, she envied

Cameron for being a virgin and she often played devil's advocate, hoping one day, Cameron would experience the sinful pleasure. Therefore, she always teased her about her choice to abstain at twenty-three years old. The fact that someone over the age of fifteen was still a virgin seemed inconceivable to Tomiko.

Cameron looked around the venue to make sure that no one overheard Tomiko's comment. "You don't have to make the announcement to everyone."

An unknown man approached Cameron, "That was hot ma'!"

"Thanks," she replied modestly.

He handed Cameron a flyer, "You should come check us out Friday night. We would love to have you."

"Alright, I will," Cameron usually received an invitation to perform at other venues after she blessed the microphone. Tomiko's offhand comment made it difficult for Cameron to enjoy her brief stardom. She turned back towards her friend, "You are so out of line," she scolded Tomiko. "How many drinks has she had?"

LaShaun shrugged her shoulders, "You know I don't pay her any attention."

"But you need to, or you wouldn't be in that sorry ass relationship with Jason." Tomiko waved her cherry stem in LaShaun's face, and LaShaun swatted at her hand. Tomiko had no filter when it came to giving her opinion to others and liquor amplified it. She was three years older than both LaShaun and Cameron,

"And back to you," she pointed her cherry stem at Cameron. "No virgin knows that much about gettin' laid and not gettin' phone calls. You are doing somebody."

"Anyway, you don't have to experience something to know about it. Some of us learn by watching others." Cameron admitted forcefully.

"Well, excuse me" Tomiko continued in response to the insidious statement.

Cameron laughed and attempted to change the subject. "I thought you stopped drinking."

"It's Corey, isn't it?" Tomiko persisted.

Cameron could not deny Corey inspired her to write the poem. He was her constant challenge and he ignited the natural gift of writing inside of her.

"...And to answer your question smarty pants, I said I wasn't getting drunk anymore, and there is a difference from having an occasional, social drink, and getting drunk." Tomiko picked up her glass to taunt Cameron and took another sip.

"The next poet is on the stage. Can you please respect the mic?" Cameron had enough of Tomiko already.

Tomiko turned to face the stage with an unfulfilled curiosity. "Yeah, I'll respect the mic, and I respect the truth as well."

"I swear," Cameron turned her attention to the stage, "you are so crass."

"Crass my ass..." Tomiko's mouth hung in mid sentence. Cameron noticed the direction of Tomiko's gaze and turned to see what captivated her attention. Tomiko and Cameron watched him approach the table, suave and seductive.

"Cameron," Gordon extended his hand. "Great show, girl! You damn near a star ain't you?"

"Hey stranger, I haven't seen you in a long time." Cameron stood to her feet and gave Gordon a hug.

"You lookin' good girl. You keepin' it together." Cameron spent the last summer at the gym trying to lose weight. She had managed to drop from a size fourteen to a ten. She was proud of her accomplishment.

"I'm trying to maintain." Cameron answered modestly.

Gordon continued, obviously impressed by what he saw, "It's always good seeing you." Gordon's smile illuminated the darkness in the Poetry Lounge and his dark complexion blended softly with the stage light.

"You, too," Cameron tried to relax, relieved Gordon's spotlight would soon be off her.

"When are we going to hook up?" Gordon continued.

Cameron felt intimidated when it came to talking to him, not because she knew him personally, but she knew him as a poet. As a poet, he brought fire to the microphone and something happened when he stepped on the stage. Cameron was not the only woman that noticed it either. He dominated the stage with his poetic craft.

"I don't know," she responded with shrugged shoulders. He made her feel like a high school girl with a crush.

"I see you on that bullshit again," Gordon replied to her vague response.

Cameron did not understand why he desired her, especially when women frequently flocked to him after his stage performances. Gordon spent the last five years writing and reciting poetry internationally.

"*What?*" Cameron embarrassingly laughed. The more she interacted with him, the more she became somewhat accustomed to his forwardness.

"You know what I'm talkin' 'bout." He placed his index finger near Cameron's jaw line and smoothly wiped his finger across her bronze toned face. "I'll catch you later, love." He read her facial expression and let out a chuckle of victory, short and seductive. His touch lingered on her cheek and she enjoyed the feeling.

Tomiko stared in a daze as Gordon made his way to the stage. "Who was *that*?"

"Who is what? Gordon," she waved her hand to minimize the encounter. Cameron tried to remain calm as she suppressed the enjoyment she felt from her run in with him.

"That's the guy you've been talking about? He's

the one that you wrote that poem about." Tomiko searched for the title of the poem, turning towards LaShaun for help, "*Damn*, what was the name of that poem?"

LaShaun looked blankly at Tomiko.

"*Ode to the Brothers*," Cameron interjected. "And I didn't actually write the poem about him. He inspired me to write the poem."

LaShaun looked around the venue as if she were waiting on someone to walk through the door, barely catching the end of the conversation between Tomiko and Cameron. They always seemed to debate with one another, and LaShaun could care less for the word tug-o-war.

Tomiko read LaShaun's facial expression and noticed her discontentment. "Jason ain't bringing his ass to no intellectually stimulating shit like this, so stop looking for him." She teased her.

LaShaun extended a middle finger toward Tomiko, "Forget you. I'm not looking for Jason."

"What's wrong with you?" Cameron asked concerned. "You seem a little out of it tonight."

"I don't know," LaShaun shrugged her shoulders.

"I've just been thinkin' a lot lately. I think I want to be with Jason."

"Well, what are you doing now?" Cameron naively asked.

"They are *cut buddies*'!" Tomiko interjected. "Come on Cam. You just got up there and did that poem, and now you are acting like you don't know what's going on. Every woman that has sex with a man for over a three-month period wants to be more than just a friend. It's natural. That's why I cut niggas off after three months, two if I can." Tomiko began sipping her drink, "I mean I used to, anyway."

Cameron looked at Tomiko with disgust. "No

more drinks for you. I'm serious."

"I already said that I'm not getting drunk, lay off me Mother Theresa."

"No," LaShaun defended Tomiko, "Tomiko's right and I don't know. I mean-I think I wanna be with him."

"I say, it's about time. You've only been the man's concubine for two years." Tomiko continued.

LaShaun rolled her eyes at Tomiko, this time feeling offended by the comment. "It's not even like that, and we haven't been seeing each other for two years yet."

"Well, tell him what you want." Cameron counseled her. "He will do one of two things: comply or leave. Either way, you got your answer. You don't wanna feel like you're committed to someone who is not committed to you. You don't even date other guys Shaun. It's like he has this hold on you. He doesn't even come around enough for you to deprive yourself of someone better."

"Well, look at you," Tomiko leaned back in her seat with disbelief and put her hands across her chest. "And why haven't you given Mr. Gordon the time of day? Too busy chasing after that dream of you and Corey being together?"

"*Alright*, that's the third time you've mentioned his name today. This is not about me." Cameron redirected Tomiko and slightly rolled her eyes.

"Who's counting?" Tomiko teased. "Okay, I'm not going there anymore tonight." Tomiko raised her hands, surrendering the idea of getting into an in depth discussion about Cameron and Corey.

"I appreciate it." Cameron continued, "Tell him Shaun. You'll feel much better when you do."

"That's right. Breathe, bitch breathe." Tomiko sipped her drink again and ended the conversation about Jason for the night.

Chapter 4 the house call

LaShaun spent the remainder of her Thursday night cleaning the apartment. Cameron was in her room asleep and LaShaun attempted to clean quietly, knowing she wanted to talk to someone about how she felt. Cameron gave her good advice, but she could not begin to understand how LaShaun had fallen for Jason. It was not just about the sex. It was everything he represented.

Jason was a local photographer and at twenty-nine, he already established himself as one of the most reputable photographers in Atlanta by working with artists nationwide. He was a dream catch for any woman, especially for LaShaun who was used to dealing with men that were a little rough around the edges, like her ex-boyfriend Andre.

LaShaun reminisced on her violent break up with Andre, which ended at Corey's apartment. Andre and LaShaun's relationship had been heading in a spiral decline before the final incident confirmed the inevitable and sent LaShaun to her breaking point.

Cameron and LaShaun were finishing their

senior year in college, and LaShaun had been dating Andre for three years, since her sophomore year in college. LaShaun woke up at one o' clock that morning to discover that Andre snuck out of the house. She immediately called Cameron.

"Cameron, wake up." LaShaun knew if she called Cameron at an early morning hour there was a chance she'd be asleep.

"Shaun?" Cameron responded in the anticipated groggy half-sleep voice.

"Yeah, it's me and I need a big time favor from you. Wake up."

"I'm up." Cameron yawned. "What's going on?"

"This muthafucka snuck out of the house and took my car."

"Andre?"

"Yes. I can't believe this asshole."

"Well, maybe he just went to the store or something." Cameron yawned, "He'll probably be back in a minute. Don't get all worried about it."

"Or maybe he has a death wish and chose me to be his angel of death."

"Shaun, there is no need to be irrational. I am sure he'll be right back. Why are you worried? Did you guys have a fight or something?" Cameron was ready to solve the problem over the phone and get back to bed.

"No, we didn't have a fight," LaShaun paused holding back her tears. She knew where Andre would be and she knew how to find him. "I need you to give me a ride somewhere."

Cameron realized that LaShaun was hurt when her voice started breaking up over the phone. "Okay, give me a minute. I'll be over there as soon as I slip something on."

Considering that Cameron and LaShaun lived in the same apartment complex, the wait would not be long. When Cameron pulled up in her Honda Civic,

LaShaun was already waiting on the front steps of her apartment building. The Honda was a gift from Cameron's father, and she had almost fallen out when he had driven it home over her Christmas break in California.

"Girl, you look crazy sittin' out here this early in the morning."

"I really don't give a damn." LaShaun had her long hair brushed back into a ponytail, wore a tattered white t-shirt, and jeans that had holes in the thighs. She looked like a woman from a 1980s rap video. All she needed was a pair of bamboo earrings, but LaShaun's eyes did not indicate that she would be having any type of party tonight.

LaShaun directed Cameron through the dark wooded streets of College Park, Georgia, a small town fifteen minutes outside of Atlanta.

"Turn here." She directed Cameron into a townhome subdivision.

"Who lives here?" Cameron asked, but LaShaun did not answer. They pulled into a parking space right by LaShaun's 1989 Oldsmobile Ninety Eight.

"You comin' in with me?"

"Yeah," Cameron agreed knowing LaShaun's question was a statement not an option. Cameron followed LaShaun to the front door of one of the townhomes and watched her bang on the door with intensity.

"You think they are going to be able to hear you with all that loud music playing?" Cameron inquired as she recognized the sound of Dr. Dre's *Chronic 2000* album penetrating the door of the townhome.

"All they do is party." LaShaun continued pounding on the door and ignoring the cold rippling her knuckles with a prickly sting.

The night air kept Cameron on her toes. She bounced from side to side trying to shake the January chill. Her California temperament had not gotten used to the painstakingly low temperatures.

"Well, I hope they answer the door soon because I might have to go back and sit in the car. It's got to be like twenty degrees out here."

Corey answered the door accompanied by a cloud of smoke that lingered from his lips toward the nostrils of the two young women waiting on the other side. Cameron and LaShaun realized that chronic was not only playing on the disc player, but also between Corey's lips. Cameron plugged her nose, while LaShaun broke the smoky trail in mid air by fanning her hands in the front of her face.

"Shaun!" Corey reached to pick LaShaun from her feet and give her a hug. "What's crackin'?"

"Your boy's head," LaShaun replied sharply while moving Corey to the side with her forearm and briskly walking past him.

"Hey, none of that domestic violence shit." Corey gazed over at Cameron and yelled out to LaShaun, "Did you tell her yet?" Corey's slanted eyes seemed to disappear as his cheekbones rose to his temple. He had the physique of an athlete. His shoulders were broad and his arms, chest and lower body well toned. Cameron could not put her finger on it, but there was something inexplicably captivating about Corey.

"Cameron that's Corey," LaShaun yelled back as if she did her part. He asked LaShaun to fix him up with Cameron after he saw them together on campus one day. LaShaun liked Corey as her friend, and loved Cameron like a sister. She did not want to cause any undue stress in her friendship with Cameron by officially introducing them. She continued to make her way towards the kitchen and bypassed a group of people sitting on the couch playing Madden.

"What's up LaShaun?" P-Body sat at the dining room table playing dominoes. He projected his voice clearly across the room in an attempt to warn Andre she was approaching him. It was too late. LaShaun already turned the corner, barely acknowledging P-Body's salutation.

"Where the fuck are my keys?" LaShaun asked in a low but authoritative voice. The tone implicated Andre needed to produce her keys in her hands without hesitation or resistance. He sat his bottle of beer near the kitchen sink and pushed himself off the counter he leaned on for balance as a young girl stepped away from him.

"'Shaun, don't come in here with no bullshit," he warned her.

LaShaun smacked him across the back of his head. "You are the one full of shit."

Andre shook his head back and forth but remained calm. "Don't put your hands on me."

"Fuck you Andre!" LaShaun put her index finger in his face, "This is the type of shit you want me to go through for the next nine months of my life? What happened to being a changed man, and not drinking and smoking anymore?" LaShaun flicked the rolled joint from behind his ear. "You are a sad ass excuse for a man."

"'Shaun, come on, I told you to quit playin'," Andre's reflexes were slow. He reached on the cabinet and picked up the joint LaShaun just popped from the side of his ear. "Don't do this shit here."

"Give me my fuckin' keys!" LaShaun extended her hands for Andre to place her keys in them.

"You know what?" Andre took the keys out of his pocket and threw them at LaShaun. The keys bounced off her shoulder and landed in the middle of the floor right between her feet. "Take yo' keys and take yo' ass home and chill out." Without any warning LaShaun took her hand and open palm smacked Andre in his face. Andre immediately grabbed her by the arms and started shaking her as if she were a stuffed doll. LaShaun kneed him in between his legs, smashing the most sensitive part of his body.

P-Body left his opponents at the domino game to respond to the chaos in the kitchen. He observed the scene from the dining room table and noticed Andre's dark face turning an infuriated red. He immediately grabbed LaShaun from behind and removed her from Andre's reach. "Put me down," she yelled out. He carried her five-feet- four-inch frame from the kitchen to the front door. One of the spectators opened the door to let P-Body out with LaShaun as she kicked and screamed for him to release her.

Cameron and Corey were still standing at the front door when P-Body passed them carrying LaShaun.

P-Body looked at Corey and signaled he needed to talk to him and both he and Cameron followed him outside. "Yo' girl is trippin' man. She slapped the shit out of Dre in there." P-Body held his hand to his face trying to hold back his smirk.

Corey looked at LaShaun. Nothing amused him about the situation. "'Shaun, I told you about that domestic violence shit. Don't bring that to my house."

"Fuck him," LaShaun continued as she panted heavily.

LaShaun stood in front of Cameron with her coat hanging from her shoulder. Cameron never witnessed her friend in such an altered state of mind. It made her nervous. LaShaun's soul seemed to vacate her body at that moment.

"What happened in there Shaun?" Cameron asked.

"Stupid ass Dre tried to play me." LaShaun spitted the words out of her mouth.

"You are outta pocket," Corey scolded LaShaun.

"Hold up," Cameron raised her hand to Corey and continued questioning LaShaun in concern. "Did he hit you?"

"Hold my drink." Corey shoved his drink into LaShaun's hands and went inside his townhome to investigate the scene. LaShaun and Andre both knew he did not allow fighting in his home.

LaShaun stood outside, calculating how she would get around P-Body and back into the apartment to finish Andre off. "Fuck him! He's in there trying to lay up with some other bitch and I'm just supposed to act like everything is cool. This is some bullshit and you know it!" She replied to Corey as he slammed the door behind him. No one understood the amount of suffering she went through contemplating if she would keep the unborn child she carried.

LaShaun began to cry out, "I hate him!" Cameron moved closer to her friend and provided her a comforting hug. "I hate him," she continued between sniffles and sobs. Cameron silently cried with her friend and began to feel the cold silent tears run down her cheeks. Cameron had no idea that LaShaun cried for two that night.

Two years passed since that night. LaShaun did not date anyone until she met Jason. Of course, she never expected to sleep with Jason. It just happened. She met him at the grocery store in her neighborhood and found out that he owned a home in the area. She started spending time with him as a friend. He did not pressure her or make any suggestions leading to intimacy. That is what she enjoyed most about their situation. His nonchalant attitude about sex transformed into a nonchalant attitude about the status of their relationship.

Now that she and Jason dated almost two years, she felt ready for a commitment from him. She wanted Jason to stay around and hoped talking about them being a monogamous couple would solidify their relationship.

In the middle of her thoughts, the doorbell rang. She quickly walked down the hall and noticed it was after midnight. She looked through the peephole and opened the door with a smile. Jason stood in her doorway with a full-length black wool coat and a black skull hat. He removed his hat and placed it across his chest to mock politeness.

"Are you busy?" he asked her.

"What are you doing here at this time of night?" LaShaun asked in a seductive voice.

"Just call me Dr. Feel Good. I'm makin' my rounds."

Chapter 5 lovers and friends

"Uhm, it smells good in here. It smells like popcorn and caramel," Cameron inhaled the warm aroma and walked in the Southern State University apartment where Josh resided.

"What are you talking about?" Josh asked while Cameron rushed passed as he closed the door.

"You made caramel popcorn." Cameron smiled and made her way through the tiny living room and into the kitchenette.

"Maybe I did and maybe I didn't," he teased. He followed her closely. When they made it to the kitchen, Cameron grabbed the bag of popcorn out of the microwave.

"Thank you so much."

"I know it's a must have for you." Josh leaned on the counter. His height looked out of place in the campus apartment. Compared to his height, the apartment looked like the dwellings for a dwarf.

"On my way over here I was hoping that you had

some because I didn't stop at the store, and I thought to myself, I don't know if I can make it a whole night without caramel popcorn," Cameron babbled.

"Well it's seven, are you ready to start or did you need some time? I know you don't like to stay up too late."

"Let's get to it," Cameron replied between bites of popcorn. "Oh, by the way, how did the interview go?"

"It went well. They scheduled me for a second interview in Philly next week." Josh answered with a confident grin.

"They're going to fly you out?"

"Yup," Josh answered casually.

"They must really want you."

"I think I pretty much got the job. The second interview is just a formality."

"What about the comp exam? Did you pass it?"

The department chairs designed the comprehensive exam, or comp, and all business administration graduates had to pass it in order to receive their master's degree.

"We're still waiting on the scores. They'll post them after finals."

"Was it hard?"

"A little, I'm not worried about it. It wasn't as bad as I thought." Josh looked at Cameron. "Are you worried about comps?" He asked in an encouraging voice.

"Yeah, who isn't? I've never been a good standardized test taker."

"It's not standardized; it's based on what we learned, and you make good grades in class so I bet you'll do fine. Just study the finals from all the major courses."

"Do you know how many classes are combined in that one test? Some of those classes I didn't even really study for them. It just was kind of common sense. I don't know all the terms, especially for those theory classes, like organization management."

"Cameron, you will do fine." Josh reassured her.

"Well, I decided that I'm going to do a thesis instead of the comp."

"Are you serious? You're going to kill yourself. How are you going to finish a thesis by next semester?"

"I don't know. There might not even be a next semester for me. I may not even finish school."

"What's going on with you Cameron? You're talking crazy. You only have one more semester to go. You can do this. I'll help you. Just don't start losing it on me."

Cameron tried to remain composed, but the pressure of graduate school was starting to make her nervous. "You're right. I'm just talking out the side of my neck. I'm going to finish. It would be dumb for me to stop right now." Cameron half-heartedly admitted, "I'm only a semester away from a master's degree."

Josh sensed Cameron's uneasiness, "Are you sure you're okay?"

"I sure am. Let's get to studying."

Josh and Cameron sat at the round wooden table with two small chairs. Cameron opened her book and started reading when she remembered her last encounter with Meagan.

"By the way, Meagan wants you to call her. She's dying to study with you." Cameron looked at Josh to see how he would respond but he continued to read his notes. "She said she had a copy of the final and she would give it to us, if we wanted it."

Josh shrugged his shoulders indicating he was not impressed.

"Josh, what's up with that? Why don't you like her?"

"She's just not my type," Josh's tone was abrupt.

"Oh, really," Cameron teased him. "Well, who is

your type, because I don't ever see you hangin' out with anyone?" Cameron paused before her next question, hoping not to offend him, "Do you like men?"

"Get the fuck out of here Cameron."

"What? I don't know. I'm just asking. I would still be your friend no matter what your sexual preference."

"Cameron, I don't like men. Okay." Josh sharply retorted. "Just lay off of me."

"Wow! I'm sorry I didn't mean to get you upset like that."

Josh turned to Cameron, surprising her, "You just don't get it, do you Cameron?" She had never seen him upset. "All this time we've spent together and you still just don't get it."

"Josh, I'm sorry. I didn't know that would offend you so much."

"No," Josh calmed himself. "I shouldn't expect you to know because I never told you." Josh leaned forward and kissed Cameron on the lips slowly. Cameron hesitantly accepted his kisses with a guilty yearning. Josh grabbed her chair and moved her closer to him. She tried to relax and embrace the sensation she felt from his embrace but the unanticipated moment made it impossible for her to become comfortable.

She stopped him just as he was sliding his hands over her breast.

"Whoa, that's enough," she sat up hastily and fixed her clothes.

For a moment, Josh and Cameron sat silently.

"What was that about?" Cameron asked breaking the silence.

"I haven't dated anyone since we started hangin' together because I'm tryin' to get with you." Josh confessed.

"*Me*," Cameron stated astonished. "I had no idea."

"You said that like it's impossible for a man to fall for you. You're beautiful Cameron." Josh stared at Cameron, "besides, there's a lot that you don't know about me."

She tried to avoid his stare, although their proximity to one another made it difficult. "I'm listening," Cameron encouraged him to talk in order to help replace the discomfort she felt from Josh's intense gaze.

"Wait here. I have something to show you." Josh went into his room and walked back out with a picture. Cameron studied it. Josh was hugging a girl that looked about her height. She had a short tapered cut and was dark brown, about the same complexion as LaShaun. "That was my girlfriend in North Carolina. We've had a long distance relationship since I came here for school. She called me at the beginning of the semester and told me that she didn't want to be with me anymore." Cameron sat in silence. "I've spent so much time working on my relationship with her. Trying to convince her that I wasn't seeing anyone else, spending money to fly, and drive, back and forth to North Carolina to be with her. When the tough times came in the relationship, my friendship with you helped me get through it."

"What's her name?" Cameron asked, gesturing to the picture.

"Candice. She was the best thing that ever happened to me. I don't understand why she wanted to call it off, but then again I do. She was ready for marriage. I'm trying to finish my degree, and I want us to be in the same state before we get married."

"It sounds like you still love her. Do you?"

"You made me realize that maybe we weren't supposed to be together. If I could have the type of feelings that I had about you, maybe I didn't love her and I was holding on to something never meant to be."

"And you think that you and I are meant to be?"

Cameron asked, not convinced at Josh's revelation.

"I don't know," Josh replied. "But I'm willing to find out."

"Josh, this is a lot to take in right now. I mean, it could be that I was just a distraction for you, so that you didn't have to deal with your real feelings for her. Because, to me, it sounds like you really love this girl." After a long pause, Cameron started smiling. "So you like black girls. Wait until Meagan finds out about this. She'll freak out."

Josh smiled and shook his head, "Please don't even mention it to her. The less she knows about me the better." Cameron and Josh sat for a minute.

"Josh, I think I'm going home now."

Josh stood to his feet, watching Cameron pack her bag. He walked her to the door. "Cameron, I hope I didn't scare you away from me because no matter what happens I always want us to be friends."

"I know." Cameron smiled and reassured him, "and we will always be friends."

"It's because I'm a white boy. Huh?"

"What are you talking about? It has nothing to do with you being white. Josh, you know me better than that. Who loves Brad Pitt more than me?"

He laughed.

Cameron needed time to process Josh's new confession. Besides, she did not want to be a rebound chick.

Chapter 6 now is not the time

Tomiko sat in the window of her hotel room overlooking downtown Chicago coated with layers of snow. Chicago's winters were beautiful, but she did not miss the cold weather. Business trips brought her back to her hometown frequently enough that she could see her mother.

She pressed the number three on her cell phone to speed dial Charlotte.

"What up, bitch!" Charlotte excitedly yelled.

"Hey Charlotte, what's up?" Tomiko calmly answered.

"You know it ain't a thing going on around here. Are you in town?" Charlotte knowingly asked.

"Yeah, I made it in earlier this morning. I was calling to see if you wanted to meet me for lunch at Giordano's."

"Yo' ass is always talking about eating at Giordano's." Charlotte laughed.

"You know that's my spot. Can you meet in an

hour?"

"Let me take care of some things right quick and I'll call you when I'm on my way."

"Alright, I'll see you there."

An hour later, Tomiko nervously waited in the restaurant, checking her watch for the time. Her heart was heavy with guilt, knowing she kept a secret from Charlotte that could change the dynamics of their friendship forever. Her cell phone rang and half her heart wanted it to be Charlotte saying she would be unable to make it. She glanced at her phone and recognized Devin's number.

"Hello," Tomiko answered somewhat agitated. She purposely avoided Devin's calls the week prior to the trip.

"Damn, baby, why didn't you tell me you were in town?" Devin responded as confidently and cocky as the day they met in high school.

"Devin, what do you want?" She introduced Devin to Charlotte over six years ago, despite the fact Tomiko already knew him intimately. In order to give the affair a proper burial, she was planning to confess to Charlotte what had been going on for the last eight years.

"Listen, I know we talked about doing this open and honest shit, but right now is not the time to tell Charlotte about you and me."

"Devin, I already told you…I need to do this for myself. I can't play these hood games with you anymore. It's not fair to Charlotte either."

"*Hood games*? Oh, I see…you from the hood but you on some bougie shit now. I don't know why 'cause you'll always be a hood rat."

"Fuck you Devin."

"I'm telling you Charlotte is not the same person you knew in middle school. The bitch is crazy, all bullshit aside. She went 51/50 on this broad just because she *thought* the hoe was jockin' me. I'm just sayin'…you my girl and I don't want to see you involved in no bullshit like that. You've been down with me from day one."

"Whatever, I can handle Charlotte and I'll deal with the consequences." Tomiko retorted dismissing Devin's perceived sincerity for selfishness.

"Just meet me tonight."

"Why the *hell* would I do that?" Tomiko asked, suspicious of Devin's motive.

"I don't want you! I just think we should talk about this and come up with a good plan, so no one is misunderstood. You don't just tell a nigga's fiancé you've been sleeping with him. That shit can ruin my family. I do care."

"*Fiancé?*" Tomiko asked, hoping she heard him incorrectly. Before Devin could respond, Tomiko noticed Charlotte entering the restaurant with a high-end designer bag on her side, and a velour designer jumpsuit. "Look I gotta go," Tomiko mumbled, rushing Devin off the phone.

"Meet me tonight," he demanded. "I'm not getting off the phone until you say yes."

"I don't have time to play with you."

"What hotel are you at?"

"Bye Devin."

"Don't tell her." Devin warned one last time.

"Bye." She slammed her flip phone together as Charlotte walked up to greet her.

Tomiko looked flushed and Charlotte noticed her uneasiness. "Tomiko, what's wrong with you?"

"Nothing, I'm sorry that was a client that I just left and I'm trying to figure out some stuff for him."

"He probably wants to take you out girl. You look sharp."

Tomiko wore a royal blue two piece tailored skirt suit that nicely outlined her curvaceous body and complimented her fair skin tone. "I must say, corporate America has treated you good. I never would have thought yo' ass would be callin' nobody's shots anywhere."

"And what is that supposed to mean?"

"Girl, you know how yo' ass used to do. Your mom spent more nights out on the porch waiting for you to come home than at any honor roll assembly." The friends shared a laugh.

"Don't act like you weren't down with me." Tomiko responded in defense.

Charlotte averted her eyes from Tomiko, barely able to look at her friend. Long gone were the days when Tomiko and Charlotte where the two most popular girls on the block. The summers spent on the porch of their homes wearing 14k gold bamboo earrings, biker shorts and t-shirts, watching Chevys pass by on gold rims, freshly painted and detailed, ringing the sound of Run DMC's, *My Addidas* from speakers heard miles before the car came into sight, were now treasured memories. Tomiko and Charlotte clearly chose different paths when the fork divided the road and the time called for them to make grown up decisions.

Tomiko made the decision to start school a little later in life than her counterparts in Atlanta. Before her grandmother passed, she prayed for Tomiko and told her to 'go to school and get her education.' She warned her not to be like her and her mother, who had children early and never went beyond high school. At nineteen, she decided to enroll in the local community college. Devin dated Charlotte for just about a year at the time Tomiko decided to go back to school. She spent two years at the community college before transferring to Brownsberry in Atlanta. One of the better decisions she made for herself in the chaos of the street life she often dabbled in while attending community college. Charlotte looked older now, as if life had beaten her up and somehow cheated her. Her beautiful long hair was held in place with an elastic band into a ragged ponytail, and her warm caramel complexion was traced with scars of war from conflicts with women and men.

"I should've followed yo' ass to school." Charlotte fixated her eyes on her coarse hands, the hands of a female muscle, a woman whose main job is to keep people in order by making them fear the consequences of disloyalty. She laughed at the thought of going to school and becoming successful like Tomiko. She could have made the same choice and Tomiko practically begged her to start college with her. Charlotte started making money fast with Devin and she was not ready to leave the lifestyle she created locally as a hustler's girl.

"Please, I don't run my job. It runs me. I barely have time to see my mom, and she is the only family I have. It just doesn't compare to being able to see your family whenever you want. And what would you do if you could hardly see Lil' Man?" Tomiko paused as the guilt of the affair resonated within her and the thoughts of the many nights she crept to see Devin plagued her mind. Tomiko had to clear her conscious or it would mentally extirpate her. "Sometimes I envy your strength, because I know it is not easy being a mother. There is no way I could do it."

Charlotte let off a sincere smile as she thought about her son, "You right-you right. I mean sometimes it just seems like I would give up these fast cars and two ways just to be normal. I've been to jail three times because I was holding dope for Devin's ass, or beating some bitch's ass for fuckin' with him, and he hasn't been to jail once."

"Charlotte, I told you about fighting over these sorry ass men and you definitely don't need to take any falls for Devin. You deserve better than that for yourself."

"I know, but I can't just think about myself

anymore. Lil' Man is getting older and he needs his father. Devin can't leave the house without him. And I know I love him Tomiko." Charlotte paused as if she were waiting for an interjection, someone to talk her out of feeling the way she did about the father of her child. "We've been talking about getting married for the past few months."

"*Married*?" Tomiko repeated as if she were hearing the possibility of Devin and Charlotte spending their life together for the first time. She wanted to reach across the table and smack some life back into Charlotte's distant and lifeless eyes. Charlotte's confidence had diminished over the past few years. Tomiko witnessed firsthand what Devin meant when he stated she was not the same. Her eyes were old, and she looked like life had already passed her by and did not plan to come back. Tomiko refused to be the one that would send her over the edge on a mass murder spree. Charlotte could be dangerous if you crossed her on the wrong street at the wrong time. "Charlotte, I'm not sure that's what you want to do."

"Of course it's what I want to do. Do you know that those two are the only reason my life has any meaning? I love them with all my heart." Her words, so passionately spoken, sent chills surging down Tomiko's back. It was sad. Tomiko couldn't imagine only being able to live for a brother that couldn't identify monogamy or love if it came and robbed him of all other emotions.

"I hear you," Tomiko reluctantly agreed.

"Good, because I want you to be my maid of honor."

Tomiko could not grasp how her moment of confession suddenly turned into a moment of riveting revelation. She sat with her mouth half opened and half smiling. Her eyes bulged in disbelief as she listened to Charlotte.

"You remember the church we always said we would get married at down the street from the high school? I'm looking there for the ceremony. It's going to be small because, well, you know I don't have many female friends. It will probably be just you and my two cousins as bridesmaids."

Tomiko's telephone rang again. She looked at the number and glanced back to Charlotte. Devin was calling her back. Although Tomiko tried her best to appear unbothered by the phone call, Charlotte noticed her eyes shifting rather quickly in a confused and frantic motion. Before Charlotte continued discussing her plans she addressed Tomiko's flustered face, "Girl answer your phone. I know you have important people calling you."

Tomiko answered it, unsure of how to play off she was talking to Devin.

"Tomiko, I really need to see you. Are you still at lunch?" Devin asked in a voice of desperation.

Tomiko rushed Devin off the phone as quickly as she could without indicating to Charlotte that the conversation remotely involved her. "Can I call you back? I'm in the middle of lunch." She put on her most professional voice. A young man brought their deep-dish stuffed pizza to the table and Charlotte grabbed the first piece, unaware of the drama unfolding in her presence.

"Don't tell Charlotte man. This shit is serious. It's not just about coming clean anymore or you clearing your conscience. I know you can't talk, but you need to call me when you are finished with lunch. That's on da' real."

"I will make a note of that and fax it over to the office first thing in the morning. Thanks." She flipped her cell phone closed and looked at Charlotte. "I apologize. These clients can be bothersome sometimes, so what were you saying?"

Charlotte gave her a proud smile. "Yeah, that's why you were supposed to fly in a day earlier, but I ain't mad at you." Charlotte continued, "Anyway, I don't want to bore you with the details. Has my cousin Keisha called you yet?"

"No, she hasn't." Tomiko responded curiously.

"I told her to call you. She is trippin'. I told her to call you about the plans because I'm trying to have it in June next year. We can all get together for the holidays, or I could just call her now."

"No, that's alright. Just tell her to call me later when you speak to her again. I just have a lot on my plate this trip."

"No doubt," Charlotte confirmed. "So are you going to be my maid of honor?"

"Yes, of course I will! I'd be honored." Tomiko did agree with Devin on one thing, now was definitely not the time to tell Charlotte anything. Her fragile state of mind did not make it easy to divulge information that could possibly send her into an emotional orbit.

Charlotte kept eating the pizza ordered and noticed Tomiko not eating at all. "Aren't you going to eat girl?"

Tomiko smirked picking up a slice of pizza and eating small bites barely able to digest all that transpired between her, Charlotte and Devin. She would revisit her approach to telling Charlotte everything but it definitely had to happen before any wedding.

Tomiko arrived at her hotel at ten that evening and immediately spotted Devin in a tan color Urban Gear sweater, a matching knit hat with Urban Gear embroidered across the front, a dark brown leather coat, and a pair of baggy jeans. He sat in the middle of the lobby waiting area. She quickly walked past as he tried to engage her in conversation.

"*Tomiko!*" He jumped off the couch when he saw her

walking past him, "Wait up, why you walkin' so fast?"

"Devin, how did you know where I was staying?"

"Your girl told me." He smiled sinisterly.

"Of course, that damn Charlotte tells you everything." Tomiko scurried across the marble floor of the hotel through the hotel lobby to the elevator banks where finally stopped to face Devin. "Please just go now."

"Tomiko, how can you play me off like this? We've been down for years. What did I ever do to you?"

Tomiko turned to press the elevator button and responded to him with an abrupt tone. *"Devin, just stop it! Okay?* This is sick. Charlotte is in love with you and I really don't feel comfortable with you coming up here like this. Let's just leave it alone. I didn't tell her. So what do you want from me?"

"Tomiko, I always wanted you but you never gave me a chance. You know that. You kept going on some bullshit 'Charlotte likes you.'" He mimicked Tomiko as a teenager. "You practically shoved yo' girl on me."

Tomiko stared at Devin, arms folded, emotionless and unmoved by Devin's recount of their relationship as teenagers. "If you didn't want to date her you could have said so; and just because I told you she liked you didn't mean you were obligated to be with her or have a child with her." Tomiko let out a frustrating sigh, "Now you're *marrying* her. I'm not doing this to her anymore. I haven't felt anything for you in years. It just kind of became a routine. I'm in town, we hook up, that's it. I'm done with the casual relationship thing. It's over."

Devin, knowing Tomiko for years, could tell by Tomiko's crossed arms and rolled eyes that she was not buying it. In desperation, he pleaded for her sympathy.

"You think this is easy for me?" He pressed his hands to his chest to draw Tomiko's attention back to him and paused to see if she still cared. "Because it's not! I always wanted it to be you, but after she had the baby, I knew I couldn't leave. It's not because I don't care. I'm just not in love with her like I was with you."

"Well you know what? Boo muthafuckin' hoo. It is time to grow up. We are not teenagers anymore. Be a man for once in your life."

Devin took a step back from Tomiko. He hadn't experienced her this way before and it caught him off guard. He didn't have a defense or come back line for her this time.

Tomiko was growing impatient with Devin's pitiful pleas. It wasn't about him, her or Charlotte any more. Tomiko couldn't look her three-year-old godson in the face without conjuring up a spiritual battle to do the right thing.

She continued on her rant, "Devin, if it's not me, it's always going to be somebody else. It's wrong. So don't sit up here and act like the shit is so deep with us and that's why you've been fucking up. You wonder why that girl is going crazy. Look at yourself."

A phone call interrupted Tomiko's frank speech.

"Tomiko." Charlotte cried out in desperation.

"Hey, wassup girl?"

"I've been trying to reach Devin for the past couple of hours, and he's not answering his phone or calling me back. I'm getting a little worried."

"Well, Charlotte, I'm not sure what you want me to do. I just got back to the hotel and I'm really tired..."

Charlotte interrupted, "Just come ride with me to check a couple of places he hangs out. I just want to make sure he's alright."

Damn, Tomiko thought. *Just what I need.* "Ok, I'll meet you at your house."

"I'm so glad you're here girl."

"Yeah, me too." Tomiko flipped her phone shut and placed it in her purse.

Devin's eyes searched her face for a clue to her changed demeanor. She turned from the elevators and began walking back towards the hotel concierge. Devin grabbed her arm, beckoning her to stay. "Tomiko, where are you going? You know I hate when you walk off from me like that."

She snatched her arm from him. "I'm going to help Charlotte." Her reply was as cold as the early-December Chicago temperature.

"...*To help Charlotte?* Man!" He exclaimed throwing his hands in the air in a surrendering gesture. "Help Charlotte do what?"

"Look for you."

The concierge observed the exchange between the two in anticipation of Tomiko's request. "Can you please have my car brought back around? Thank you!"

The concierge politely nodded and picked up the phone to notify the valet.

Tomiko walked out the door and turned to Devin standing beside her while she awaited her rental car. "Devin, you need to be at home, not here."

The valet opened the driver side door for her and she got in her car. The events of the day brought about another epiphany for Tomiko; there was no way she could move back to Chicago.

As she drove off, she peered out of her rearview mirror. She saw Devin, long faced and puppy dog-like, pulling his cell phone out of his pocket. She hoped her words finally reached the deep place in Devin's chest where most humans had a heart. Maybe tonight's man search would not be long after all.

"I'm just too old for this shit," she said to herself.

Chapter 7 the unwelcomed guest

After the popular video for one of the newer artists, Young-T, rotated the airwaves for the third time in a matter of an hour, Cameron quickly grabbed the remote and turned the television set completely off. She could lose her mind, and self-esteem, if she looked at one more video featuring half-naked women with long weaves, and total body weight that was as big as her left thigh. Not to mention she was just about disgusted at the monotony and subject content of music videos and music in general. However, she would find herself swaying her hips and bobbing her heads to songs when she did not care for the lyrics.

Cameron let out a deep sigh, "I am pitiful."

She looked at her textbook that sat on the couch with the pages turned open and her notebook beside it. The concept of studying right now did not sit well with her. She had taken off the whole week from her part-time job to study for finals. However, not being busy proved to be a handicap for Cameron. She was use to

Josh being around to keep her focused. It was difficult for her to stay on task for a prolonged period on her own. Just when she picked up her book, the doorbell rang.

She stood on her tiptoes and looked through the peephole. The most infamous of all unexpected guests, Jason, stood at the door. In his black ski hat, ski jacket and leather gloves. Jason looked like a thief. Cameron stood on the other side of her door wearing green scrubs and house shoes. She could see the cold coming from his mouth while he rubbed his hands together.

She opened her door with an unsettling agitation. "Can I help you?"

"Cameron!" Jason smiled and gave her a hug as if she were his closest friend. It had been over three months since he last saw her, but she was not thrilled. Jason was a waste of time for LaShaun. Cameron tried to figure out what made LaShaun fall for him the way she did, and why did he not use his charm for good?

Jason was not overly attractive. He was slim and dressed in upscale name brands, a typical tawdry man with an excessive amount of money and time on his hands.

"You look good Cameron. You lost a lotta weight. You smokin' crack or somethin'?"

"Is yo' mama smokin' crack?" Cameron quickly replied rolling her eyes and closing the door behind him. Comments like those made Cameron want him to leave expediently.

"You need to get you some." Jason answered in rebuttal.

"And you need to get you some business." Cameron walked back into the living room to reclaim her previous position on the couch, "What do you want Jason?"

"I can't come by and holla at my friend?" He sat on the couch next to Cameron.

"You need to be hollerin' at your girl, not me." Jason seemed to be under the impression that every woman adored him and did not mind having him around.

"That's not my girl," Jason reminded her.

"Well, you sure act like she's your girl. I bet you don't tell her that." Cameron did not condone the way he came in and out of LaShaun's life and she particularly did not care for his condescending innuendos.

"I just came to get the stuff I left here the other night." Jason boasted pulled his slacks over his belly, and stuck out his chest.

"What do you mean, the other night?" Cameron asked unaware of Jason's late night visit.

"I guess she doesn't tell you everything." Jason laughed and made his way to LaShaun's bedroom.

Cameron read her textbook while Jason went through LaShaun's bedroom. He came out of the room with a small tank top. "What is this?" Jason asked, holding the top between the tips of his fingers.

Cameron looked at him disturbed, "It's a tank top."

"Yeah, but whose is it? LaShaun can't fit her chest in this." LaShaun had a chest that was large in comparison to her stature, but she loved wearing clingy tops that cut low around her breast.

"Don't come in here disrespecting my roommate, okay?" Cameron grew impatient with him. She jumped off the couch, snatched the shirt from his hand and walked into LaShaun's room. "Just get what you came for and be out." Cameron sat at the bedroom door to police Jason.

He looked around the room and then looked back at Cameron. "Can I ask you something?"

Cameron rolled her eyes to the top of her head, crossed her hands over her chest and prepared for another sarcastic remark. "What, Jason?"

"What's going on with LaShaun? She seemed funny last night."

"What do you mean, like 'giggly' funny or like 'something's wrong' funny?"

"Like she had something on her mind and she didn't know how to tell me."

"Why didn't you ask her?"

"I did, but she just kept shruggin' her shoulders and saying, 'nothing'." Jason imitated a female's voice.

Cameron laughed at the inane imitation of her roommate, "Well, I don't know."

"I think she's falling in love with me," Jason replied cockily.

"Please! What makes you think she's in love? She doesn't even see you enough to be in love with you."

"All you need is Mr. Johnson once a month. That's enough to get you sprung, girl. You didn't know?"

"No, and I'm not curious to find out."

Jason picked up a small traveling bag and placed it under his arm. "Well, I'm gone. I'll see you later Cam."

"I did not give you permission to call me by my nickname."

"Get that chip off your shoulda, you'll be alright." Jason let himself out of the apartment.

"Lock the door!" Cameron yelled as Jason exited. She dialed LaShaun's work number as soon as the door slammed shut. She felt LaShaun should be more careful about her feelings when dating Jason and not just give her energy to the first man that became available to her.

Chapter 8 who can play the game

"Girl, you ain't shit."LaShaun's coworker, Reese, casually greeted her as she walked into her office.

LaShaun could here Reese's bangles approaching her before she turned around from her desktop computer monitor to respond. Reese stood in LaShaun's peripheral, silently demanding attention, She folded her arms folded; and propped herself against the corner of LaShaun's desk.

"Why didn't you call me to go to the poetry thing-ama-jig, last night?" Reese stood five feet eight inches tall and used her hands, neck, and hips to express herself. Reese convinced everyone around her that she was destined to be a supermodel and she hung around people, especially men, she thought could help her advance in her modeling career. "Shaun, you are just wrong."

"Why am I wrong, Reese?" LaShaun began entertaining her friend and co-worker.

LaShaun truly loved Reese, but only take her in

doses because her personality was somewhat grandiose. LaShaun ignored her and continued to work on the team's weekly production reports. They worked for Southern National Bank, a credit card company. As a team leader, her main concern was assuring her team met their weekly account acquisition quota.

"You know I wanted to go to the little poetry place and you didn't even call me." Reese pouted.

"I told you that it's every Thursday night. It's not my fault you're too busy to hang out with ya' girl. And Cameron was off the hook last night."

"You could've reminded me." Reese helped herself to the peppermints sitting on LaShaun's office desk.

"You wanna hang out tonight?"

"I don't know. I need to check my calendar, because, you know, things may be working out for a sistah tonight."

"Things like Calvin?" LaShaun teased.

Calvin was an editor for a local magazine and an entertainment manager. Although he was the main object of Reese's desire this week, she always left room in her Rolodex to add new entries.

"Please believe it!" Reese replied as she did her rendition of the hip-hop dance known as the Tootsie Roll.

"Why are you still dealing with him? I thought he wasn't acting right."

"What man do you know acts right? Girl, it's not meant for them to act right. It is meant for us to teach them how and how not to act." Reese leaned on LaShaun's desk. "Every man needs training--including your friend Jason."

Reese transformed into an erudite person and informed LaShaun on the basic rules of life.

"You know why men love a woman that plays hard to get?" Reese waited for a response from LaShaun.

LaShaun looked at her with anticipation. Reese typically did not allow room for comments when she got into her instructor mode. "No, Reese, why do men like a woman that plays hard to get?"

"Anything that a man has to work for, to him, is worth keeping. If it's too easy, there's no challenge, no competition, and I know playing hard to get works 'cause whenever I switch it up on Calvin, he comes around full force. It's just one of the things you have to do to keep your relationship alive. Men do not like monotony. Shit, most of them don't like monogamy. Something about the mono prefix scares them, one-on-one, you and me, 'mono y mono'. Sometimes you gotta make them feel a little insecure. Like I don't have to be here and I will leave yo' ass if you continue to act the way you actin'. You have to punish them. It's a part of the training process."

"Okay 'Two Can Play That Game.'" LaShaun laughed, "You know you sound like Vivica Fox in that movie."

"And you know it," Reese bragged. "Did she not get her man at the end of the movie? Oh yes she did, and you know why? She kept him in suspense and he loved her. When men are not acting right, you have to take away whatever means the most to them. Sometimes you may have to restrain from calling them, others you may have to restrain from sexing them, or cooking for them. Something unique you bring to the relationship that you know he enjoys. Once they notice they shit ain't there anymore, they will start to miss it. That is, if you have a good man, and if you do they will always come back."

"And if you don't have a good man?"

"If you don't, you shouldn't want him anyway."

LaShaun began nodding her head in agreement, "I can feel you on that one."

"Now, that one is for free. If you need more advice I got to charge you at the nominal rate of twenty-five dollars a minute."

They both began to laugh. LaShaun's phone rang and she looked at the caller display screen, "Oh this is my roommate, hold on while I take this call."

"Girl, I do have work to do. Let's meet up for lunch, okay?"

LaShaun shook her head to confirm the lunch date and immediately picked up the phone, "Hey Cameron, what's up?"

"Trying to figure out what is wrong with Jason," she suggestively answered. "You know your boy came by today."

"*Jason?*" LaShaun asked, surprised.

"Yes."

"What did he want?"

"The stuff he left over here the other night," Cameron sat in silence, waiting for an explanation from LaShaun.

"Oops," LaShaun replied.

"Yeah, oops…I'm glad to know we have such a close friendship. I bet Reese knows he came by already."

"I haven't told anyone about that night."

"Well, he is crazy and you need to tell him that he should call before he comes by because I sure wasn't expecting him."

"Cameron, I will tell him next time we talk. Don't get all upset about it." LaShaun was in no mood to hear a lecture from anyone else about what she should do with Jason.

"Thank you. I'll call you later."

"Bye."

LaShaun hung up the phone and scratched her head in amazement and confusion. A few months ago, she could not get him to stop by without pulling teeth, and now he was coming by on his lunch break.

She started to draft an email but realized she may do more damage than good. She wanted Jason to feel comfortable stopping by, and she certainly did not want this to hinder any progress they were making in their relationship.

"Hello, this is LaShaun."

"'Shaun, are you busy?" Jason's voice sounded hurried.

"Not really, why?"

"Why is your roommate sittin' at home in her pajamas? She doesn't have a job anymore?"

"Yeah, she has a job. She just didn't feel like going into work today."

Jason was always trying to figure out what was going on with someone else.

"Well, she should at least get up and scrub her ass. She's sitting around as if she lost her best friend. Where is her man at?"

"Jason?" Her voice showed her discontentment in him wasting her time with his nosiness.

"Huh?"

"You are being just a little bit too nosy. Didn't you just leave from over there?"

"Yeah."

"So why didn't you ask her all these questions you're asking me?"

"Because she would have cursed and threw me out the apartment."

LaShaun laughed because Jason was not exaggerating. "Okay, so why are you asking me?"

"Alright, I'm about to go." Jason hung the phone up before LaShaun could even say bye. When she laid the phone back on the receiver, the phone rang again.

She took a deep breath and answered the phone, "LaShaun Johnson speaking."

"Hey Shaun, it's me." Cameron sheepishly responded.

"What's up?"

Cameron and Jason were bothering her the way two little kids home from school on summer vacation bothered their mother at work; they infectiously called with no regard for her responsibilities at work. She still had to finish productivity reports before lunch.

"I just wanted to apologize if I had a bit of an attitude earlier. You know I'm cool with Jason. I just would prefer he called you when he planned on stopping by."

"You have every right to feel the way you do and I understand." LaShaun paused, leaving an awkward silence over the phone. "Well I am about to get back to work. Are you going to need anything before I get home?"

"No, I should be fine. If I really need something, I'll get my lazy butt up and grab it. I mean, I am off today."

"It must be nice to be able to take time off to study. Hell, I should really go back to school and get my Master's."

"It's not as good as it looks. Believe me." Cameron warned her. "I'll talk to you later."

LaShaun hung up the phone knowing that Jason had a habit of being a bit overbearing at times. She drafted the email but did not send it. She needed to address Cameron's concerns without causing any friction in her and Jason's delicate and slow progressing relationship, but how would she tell him?

Chapter 9 when love calls

Cameron arrived to the Financial Management final exam thirty minutes before the start of class to get in some last minute cramming. When she arrived, the lecture hall was barren to her surprise. Fifteen minutes into her review of her notes, the class became increasingly louder as it filled with the normal occupants.

Josh walked in the classroom and sat in the chair a row behind Cameron. "What happened to you this week?" Josh whispered to Cameron.

Cameron jumped at the sound of a voice other than the one in her head repeating formulas for present and future values.

"Josh, I just needed time to study on my own."

"I didn't mean to make you feel uncomfortable."

"Can we talk about this after the test?" Cameron turned to him with a stern look, "I really need to concentrate."

"That's cool. I'm getting the picture." Josh sat

back in his seat.

Cameron rolled her eyes, "Josh, don't even go there."

Tony walked in the classroom and sat down right next to Cameron. He diffused the tension in the room and it relieved her to see him.

"Hey Pookie," he kissed her on the cheek.

"We'll talk after class," Cameron whispered back to Josh.

"Did I interrupt something?" Tony asked after he noticed the tension between Josh and Cameron.

"You're fine." Cameron placed her hand on Tony's shoulder, encouraging him to stay next to her.

"Okay," the professor demanded the attention of the classroom. "This test will take the whole two hours. I don't expect you to complete the entire test, but I do expect you to try." He handed out a stack of tests to the beginning of each row. "Be sure that there is at least one seat space next to you. There should be a student in every other seat."

Cameron rubbed her hand on her hair that she had swooped into a ponytail for ease this morning. She had thrown on her most comfortable pair of sweatpants and a sweatshirt. She sat in the lecture hall feeling ready for the task of mastering her final exam.

"Okay, everyone, pass your test forward." Mr. Jameson demanded after two hours passed. His announcement prompted pencils slamming on desktops and loud sighs across the classroom.

"*Shit!*" one student blurted out; it incited others to laughter.

Cameron was relieved she answered every question on the exam. She packed her bags and turned around towards Josh to ask him how he did. Cameron only found an empty seat behind her.

"How do you think you did?" Tony asked Cameron as she blankly started at the seat behind her.

"Me?" Cameron looked back towards Tony who helped her escape her trance. "I don't know. You can never tell how well you do on these things until you get the grade back."

"Well, I'll see you next semester. I'm outta here on the next flight to LA."

"I'll be leaving soon to go home myself." Cameron responded nonchalantly.

"Call me when you get home. I may be up your way this holiday."

"I'll be sure to do that."

"Bye," Tony scurried out of the classroom.

Cameron walked up the stairs of the classroom, not knowing how to feel about Josh's unexpected disappearance. When she opened the door of the lecture hall, she spotted Josh sitting in a seat by the coffee bar. She walked towards him, and was surprised to see Meagan headed in the same direction with two cups of coffee in her hands. Cameron continued her route to meet up with Josh.

"Hey," she greeted Josh and his newfound friend.

"Hey girl," Meagan turned towards Cameron and put on her million dollar seal-the-deal smile.

"Josh, are you really busy? I need to talk to you."

"I was just about to have a cup of coffee with Meagan. You're more than welcome to join us." Josh stared at Cameron, knowing how she felt about Meagan's presence. She would rather do a nude dance in the rain than share a coffee break with her.

"I think I'll pass. I'm not really a big coffee drinker." *Not today anyway*, she thought. "I guess I'll see you guys around." Cameron turned towards the door to make her exit.

She walked down the stairs in front of Manor Hall and made her way to the bus stop in front of the building.

Josh appeared next to Cameron shortly after she settled at the bus stop. "How do you think you did on the test?"

"I don't know," Cameron answered very shortly.

"It was kind of hard," Josh continued, in an effort to ease the tense laden conversation.

"I couldn't tell with the way you rushed out of the classroom," Cameron gave Josh the stare down. "How was the coffee?"

"Not as good as coffee with you," Josh complimented her. "Since when did you stop drinking coffee anyway?"

"The day you asked me to share a cup with Meagan."

Josh laughed, "She is pretty obnoxious, but she knows how to show somebody that she cares."

"Josh, you know I care about you. Just because I can't reciprocate the feelings that you have for me does not mean I don't care."

"I just wanted to know how you felt Cameron!" Josh exclaimed. "I put myself out there and it took *this* for you to even talk to me straight about the way you were feeling."

"I just don't see how you and I could work. You're leaving school and starting a new life, and I still have a semester to go."

"Cameron, you're making excuses. I hate when you do that, but I understand if you're not feeling me. I'm not pressuring you to have the same feelings for me that I have for you. I want us to stay friends and if my feelings for you are going to drive you away, then I'll try to stop feeling the way I do. But don't just completely stop talking to me."

"I'm sorry. I just didn't know what to say after...."

"You don't have to say anything. I'm leaving in a couple of days to go back to North Carolina. I hope that

I'll have heard something from Merchants by then. I probably won't come back here, unless someone calls me for an interview or a job offer." Josh stuck out his hand, "I just need to know that we are still friends."

"Of course were still friends," Cameron reached over to receive his hand and smiled. He pulled her closer to him and embraced her with a hug.

"Good, cause it's freezing out here. Let me give you a ride home."

Cameron sighed loudly as she sat across from her two friends in the dim Poetry Lounge for their Thursday night ritual. "I think I may have really messed up."

"How?" LaShaun asked.

"I think I may have let a really good guy go."

"Who, Josh?" Tomiko assumed.

"How did you know about Josh?"

"Cameron, it doesn't take a rocket scientist to see the chemistry the two of you have, and let's face it, your other male prospects are almost nonexistent."

"Excuse me," Cameron was insulted, "but how do you figure that?"

"Let's see, we got people we hear about but never see, that would be Corey. We got Gordon, who is just out of your league. Then we got that fine ass white boy, Josh, who obviously has feelings for you. You can't spend that much time with someone of the opposite sex without developing some sort of feelings."

"I admit, when I first met him, I may have looked at Josh once or twice like that, but then I snapped back to reality. There's no way we could work. He's just not my type."

"Do you have a type?" LaShaun argued.

"Yes, I do." Cameron paused, "I think."

"Oh," LaShaun looked at Tomiko and teased. "She likes the thuggish ruggish bone type."

"Anyway, I can't help it if I like them a little rough around the edges. I like a manly man." Cameron balled her hands into a fist and pulled them in towards her torso to flex her muscles.

"It's okay, everyone goes through that stage. But let's face it, you can't marry a thugged out ass nigga. They ain't tryna' take care of nobody but they three kids and three baby mamas." Tomiko added.

"Tomiko you are wrong," Cameron said playfully. "How can you say that about the brothas?"

"I'm not telling you what I heard. I'm telling you what I know."

LaShaun chimed in, "Why does it seem like we always fall for the bad boys anyway?"

"It's their sex appeal, you know? They have a confidence that other men just don't." Cameron dazed off thinking about what first attracted her to Corey. "They make you feel safe. Every woman wants to feel safe."

"Oh, and ain't nothing like a thugged out New Yorker." LaShaun agreed.

"Girl, are you crazy? California men have it, hands down. Sexy, laidback, but you know they will jack somebody up if they cross them the wrong way." Cameron retorted.

"Well all I'm saying is those thugged out niggas will get you in trouble every time." Tomiko interrupted, "There is nothing wrong with having a man that just knows how to take care of a woman. He doesn't necessarily have to be a thug."

"I think that all black men got it in them," LaShaun responded.

"Not all of them. Speak for yourself, because Michael ain't got it."

"Tomiko, only you would meet a black man that is a straight corn ball." LaShaun teased her friend.

"I definitely don't want someone that only knows

the streets." Cameron continued to justify her position, "I just want a gentleman that has a little thug in him. He needs to know how to flip between those personalities. I don't want him to lose a job and lose his mind, like he's going to commit suicide and kill the family because he's never experienced hard times. I want him to have an attitude like, 'I'll do whatever I need to do to take care of my family.'"

"*Legally?*" Tomiko responded sharply.

"Whatever." Cameron's voice trailed off as she stopped debating with her friends.

Yusef approached there table, "Girl talk, it's a mystery. Girl talk, are they talkin' 'bout me?" Yusef danced and sang the eighties song around the table. After a short laugh, he turned to Cameron. "You're up next. Did you bring the heat?"

"Did I ever?" She responded confidently.

He winked at her and walked off.

"I just hope I didn't make the biggest mistake of my life. I don't want to regret it." Cameron pushed her seat from the table and Tomiko grabbed her arm.

"Girl, I know I taught you better. A diva never lives with regrets. If you're thinking about it, you better say something to him."

Cameron rose from her seat and headed towards the stage as Yusef introduced her.

"Allow me to introduce a woman who really needs no introduction, as a matter of fact, I want ya'll to start clapping right now. Give it up for Cameron the Chameleon!"

Cameron grabbed the microphone from Yusef as he handed it to her. "My girls and I were just sittin' at the table talkin' about the brothas, and I thought it would be fitting to share this poem tonight. It's called Ode to the Brothas. Is that alright?" The crowd replied with a thunderous applause, encouraging Cameron to recite her work.

"I'm sitting, I'm sitting here contemplating, I wanna be another.

I wanna leave this five three size ten frame, I wanna be another.

I wanna sit on a stoop and grab my balls as we talk about shooting basketball.

I wanna rhyme and joke as we talk about folk

And have a sexiness about me that can't be explained

People would try to figure out how I reigned as King supreme in the Garden of Eden.

I wanna be cocoa brown, caramel, honeysuckle, high hue

With people hanging on to everything I say and do.

I wanna leave this double standard and handle myself in any manner I choose.

Rather I wanna have sex tonight or call it a night it really wouldn't matter.

They say that women have all the power but I beg to differ.

Ask any man how many nights he stayed up singing I miss her.

I want to escape this five-three size ten frame,

I wanna be called by another name.

Whether it be Ramon, T-bone, anything but Tyrone.

I wanna dominate the stage have people saying in a rage

Yeah you know his mode of slang

'Cause he be scoop doop a doopin, beat box-in, freestylin'

Charmin' 'em, harmin' 'em, lovin' 'em, leavin' 'em, keepin' 'em, peepin' 'em, freakin' 'em, speakin' 'em, playin' 'em, swayin' 'em, and disarrayin' 'em,

With a melodic and hypnotic voice

Not speaking erotic and still making the ladies moist

With his stage presence, his very essence and distinguished choice of…words.

I don't know if I mentioned it before or if you heard

But I wanna be another.

I wanna leave this five-three size ten frame and be

another.
I wanna transform into a six-two, I thought you knew
And if you don't you better ask somebody how I do.
Because brothas, I don't know about you but I've been
contemplating.
And all this I would do just to be that much closer to
you,
But until then I'm sitting here watching you.
I've become another.
Thank you, thank you for letting me enter the mind of a
brotha."

Chapter 10 let's get married

As Tomiko walked into Michael's split-level loft, the aroma of sautéed shrimp hit her nostrils. Michael knew shrimp was her favorite. Tomiko stepped over the threshold from his high rise's hallway into the main foyer and turned her back towards him cuing him to remove her jacket. As he grabbed the back of her jacket collar, he kissed her on the nape of her neck. She loosely shook her shoulders to let her coat fall to her hips while Michael admired her designer dress with a low cut back. It fell nicely over her body. The sounds of Coltrane played in the background and complimented the ambiance perfectly. She expected nothing less from Michael.

"You look stunning," Michael whispered in her ear.

Tomiko smiled meekly. He hung her coat on an oak coat rack that blended well with his hardwood floors. Tomiko's heels seductively tapped the floors as she made her way into the living area and on to the couch.

Tomiko fit into Michael's future career and personal goals perfectly. She was smart and ambitious. He knew a woman of Tomiko's caliber would keep him motivated. He knew it from the first day he met her. Aside from her striking beauty, which she inherited from her Creole roots, Tomiko was well spoken. When he took her to events, he did not have to cater to her while he networked and it made him confident in her. However, Tomiko did not let her guard down easily in relationships. Michael found the challenge surprisingly attractive.

"I see you got a new painting," Tomiko broke the silence. She felt Michael's panoramic stare all over her body and it aroused her. She had to change the pace of the night or she would become Michael's appetizer. The soft brush of his lips against her skin still lingered on her neck and it created a sexually charged energy she attempted to dismiss by taking the focus off her. Michael was out of the doghouse, but he kept apologizing. He wanted to prove to Tomiko that he could support her in any endeavor she chose, including celibacy. Even if he desired to fully embrace her in his arms tonight and finish the gentle kisses he started at the door.

"You like it? I brought it at the last National Black Arts Festival. It's an oil painting." Michael looked at the mural, proud of his accomplishment. He supported a local black artist and paid homage to jazz with the black and white painting. It depicted a jam session between a saxophonist and pianist.

"It's nice. I imagine that set you back a couple of grand."

"Well it's the original, so it cost me a little, but it's perfect for the spot. Don't you think?" Michael smiled charmingly as he handed Tomiko a glass of champagne.

"Perfect." Tomiko sipped her champagne and tipped her glass toward Michael, "Thanks."

"Do you remember what you said to me when we first met?'

"No," Tomiko shook her head and replied. "I really don't remember that was like five years ago." She laughed in embarrassment. Her early twenties were here socializing years and an adjustment period for her. She had just come from a fast-paced street life in Chicago to the slower flow of the south.

"I introduced myself to you while you were waiting for Cameron outside of the business building and you turned and looked at me and said, 'Do I know you?'" Michael laughed thinking about the encounter. "And I said to myself, yep she's the one."

"Michael, stop, I wasn't that bad."

Michael sat beside her and placed his arm around her shoulders, "Tomiko, I just want you to be happy. I know you have been through a lot in life and I just want you to know, you can relax now. I'm here for you."

"Is dinner ready?" Tomiko interrupted him by standing up and pulling at her perfectly placed dress.

Michael dropped his head, surrendering the moment to Tomiko. "Yeah, uh…are you ready to eat?"

"Definitely," Tomiko lead the way to the kitchen.

Dinner was already cooked and Michael set the table with the place settings for dinner. He did not use fine china, but he used the good dinner sets, all white, just like they use in restaurants. He even placed the silverware properly on the table; dinner fork to the left, knife and spoon to the right.

Tomiko observed this man serving her. She had to admit that she was quite impressed with him sharing his craftiness in the kitchen, but her mind drowned out the pleasantries she felt for the moment with one thought: *How long could it last?*

Michael took the dinner plates to the kitchen where he placed the main entrée on them near the stove. He removed the angel hair pasta from the boiling water, dumped it in a stainless steel colander and ran cold water over it. He laid the pasta on the plates and added shrimp scampi on top. He waited a long time for him and Tomiko to embark on a relationship again. They had reunited during a business conference for black professionals. While Tomiko was an undergrad at Brownsberry, Michael was finishing his Master's in Architecture at Malbury College, but he later dropped out to start his own business. They dated for three months, but Tomiko found no interest in him. Tomiko completely captivated Michael. She avoided him for the rest of his matriculation in the graduate program, but he thought about her frequently.

Tomiko wanted a man that could deliver in those days. A man that could whisk her away and take her on a weekend trip to Miami at moment's notice, a spontaneous shopping spree, a man that could drown her with instant gratification, in the most materialistic way possible. She knew this was the reason she and Michael did not make the mark on the compatibility chart during their college years. He had the qualities of a good husband and she was not in the market for one. She disliked the thought of marriage, and being with an average person just did not do it for her.

Michael had not changed, except he had more of his own money now. He was from a well-to-do family and always had a comfortable lifestyle. Michael thought it was senseless to spend money frivolously while he was trying to establish a financial legacy, the way his father did for his family. After a couple of multi-million dollar building projects and a budding consulting career, he felt more comfortable about spending but still handled his finances with economically sound decision making.

Michael placed the meals on the table and sat down across from Tomiko. Michael waited for Tomiko to take her first bite.

"How's dinner?" Michael plopped a jumbo size shrimp into his mouth and savored the garlic taste.

"It's great. You really went all out." Tomiko rubbed her hands on the white linen napkin on her lap. Michael's fine dining simulation met Tomiko's approval.

Tomiko noticed Michael staring at her as she

twirled angel hair pasta around her fork. *"What?"*

"Nothing," Michael answered in an amazed and flabbergasted way. This was the woman of his dreams.

"Okay-" Tomiko ate her fork full of pasta.

"I mean, I'm just admiring how beautiful you are."

"That's rude. I'm trying to eat and your staring at me is making me uncomfortable. You eat your food." Tomiko snapped at him.

Michael threw his hands up, "Fine." He picked his plate up, turned toward the window overlooking the downtown Atlanta skyline and began eating out of his plate while holding it in his hand.

She laughed, "You are a fool."

"If I can't look at you, I'll just eat like this." Michael continued eating with his back turned to her.

"Michael, turn around." She insisted apologetically.

He did as she commanded. Tomiko did have a good time with him. He knew how to make her laugh and he understood the importance of the finer things. He had a few custom tailored suits in his closet, and she could appreciate his style.

"Are you going back home for Christmas?" Michael restarted the conversation.

"I don't want to but last time I spent Christmas in Atlanta, I was alone. All my girls went back to their hometowns and I was stuck at home watching all sorts of Christmas stories. It made me homesick."

"Why not spend Christmas with me?"

"No, I can't stay. My mom would be devastated."

"Send for her," Michael said. "We can all have Christmas here."

"Michael, that's a little too much for us." She tried to place another piece of shrimp in her mouth when Michael stood and walked toward her. He grabbed her hand and she dropped the fork on her plate. He lifted her from her seat by her waist. "Michael, what are you doing? I'm trying to enjoy my dinner." Tomiko leaned on his forearm for balance.

"I was going to wait for a time when all of our family would be together, but I can't hold this any longer." Michael led her to the middle of the living room, knelt down on one knee and took a small black velvet jewelry box from his pocket. "Tomiko, I'd like you to make me the happiest man alive." He opened the jewelry box, "Will you marry me?"

Aw shit, Tomiko thought and placed her hand on her forehead. *Why couldn't he just want sex and leave it at that?* She stood speechless and stared at the brilliant marquis cut diamond ring. The stone that Michael presented sat in a platinum band and was much bigger than any karats in her other jewelry.

Michael stood to his feet, and examined the ring that Tomiko stared at without any emotion. "What's wrong?"

"Michael, how long have you been planning this?"

"I don't know-I mean I knew that I wanted to be married one day, and now I know it's you that I want to be with. Is that so wrong?"

"It's *wrong* that you never mentioned how you felt before now. I am not a business deal. You don't just sign on the dotted line when it comes to marriage. It's not something you take lightly…it's *forever.* You're supposed to plan with the person you are thinking about marrying. You don't just walk in the door with a ring in your hand and spring the question on them one day."

"Tomiko, I know we've only been back together for six months, but it didn't take me long to know that I want to spend the rest of my life with you. I've known it since I saw you walk across the promenade going into the student center at Brownsberry."

"I don't know…" Tomiko shook her head in disbelief and paced back into the dining area, away from Michael.

Michael interrupted Tomiko before she could

completely reject him, "Just tell me you'll think about it."

She quickly turned around to face him. "Michael, everything is so *urgent* with you. This sort of thing takes time."

"That is exactly what I'm asking you to do. Take your time and think about it." Michael walked towards Tomiko and took her left hand; he gently placed the ring on her finger. She didn't fight Michael as he slid the ring on her finger. It glistened beautifully on her hand.

Michael was offering her what any woman would desire in his eyes, a lifetime with him. Whether he previously discussed it with her or not, Tomiko could not take this romantic gesture and commitment from him.

"I guess we're supposed to make passionate love after this." Tomiko said, her voice dripping with sarcasm. She hoped that Michael was not going through the trouble of proposing just to have sex with her.

Michael smiled in an insulted manner, "Tomiko, come on. I know you know me better than that. I'm not asking you to give anymore than I'm willing and I am definitely not hard up."

Tomiko did not know anything right now. What woman would turn down such a brilliant piece of jewelry? She would be the envy of all women, at least all the women she knew, even if she wore it for a couple of days.

Tomiko walked up the steps to the second level of the apartment building where Cameron and LaShaun lived. She used her spare key to open the door. When she walked in, she went straight into the living room where she saw Cameron sitting on the couch in a sports bra and workout pants.

Cameron sipped on a fruit smoothie as she watched television. When Tomiko entered the room, Cameron noticed her despondence as she stood in the walkway between the living room and the kitchen with her hands in her pockets.

"Uh-oh, what's wrong?" Cameron sat up to make room for Tomiko to sit down.

"Nothing." Tomiko walked to the couch and slumped down next to Cameron.

"Yeah, something is wrong." Cameron grabbed the remote, turned off the television, and watched Tomiko carefully. "I haven't seen you like this since you found out they were taking the late night grill out of the cafeteria in the dormitory."

Tomiko lifted both hands to her face and revealed her engagement ring to Cameron for the first time.

"Oh my gosh!" Cameron clutched her chest, as if she gasped for air. Cameron started playfully hitting Tomiko with the tips of her fingers.

"You've been holding out on your girl. Michael bought you this?" Cameron snatched Tomiko's hand and stared at the gem. "Don't answer," Cameron interjected. "I'm going to get LaShaun." Cameron jumped to her feet, off the couch and made her way to LaShaun's bedroom.

Tomiko tried to stop her by hollering behind her. "No, don't call her!"

The next sound she heard was LaShaun shouting. "You are lyin'!" Tomiko heard a loud thump on the floor, which was obviously LaShaun rolling out of her bed and making her way into the living room.

Cameron plopped on the couch right next to Tomiko. LaShaun came out of her room two steps behind Cameron.

"Let me see it," LaShaun demanded with sleep still in her eyes and her hair sticking straight up on top of her head.

Tomiko raised her hand in a slow lifeless motion to let LaShaun see the ring.

"Ooooh, now that is a nice ring." LaShaun put her hand to her mouth to hide the gleefulness of seeing the piece of jewelry.

"I'm not keeping it." Tomiko interjected with

sternness.

Dead silence fell over the room.

"What did she say?" LaShaun sarcastically asked.

"You're not what?" Cameron asked. "You are kidding right?"

"I'm not keeping it." Tomiko repeated with confidence. "You guys know I don't love Michael. I can't marry him-I just can't. It would be for all the wrong reasons. Why is it so urgent for him to marry me anyway?"

"Maybe because he loves you Tomiko and sees something in you that you haven't allowed yourself to see." Cameron was a hopeless romantic. She believed in love. "I mean, you act like you are just the devil reincarnated or something. You are a great person and you would make a great companion for somebody. Don't let your hang-ups about love block your blessings for a husband."

"Amen," LaShaun snapped her fingers.

"See, that is the point. A husband for me right now is not a blessing. It's something I don't want-I don't want to be responsible for someone else's happiness, or sadness."

"You are one silly lady," LaShaun interrupted. "If you let that man go, you are crazy. I thought that out of all of us, you had the most sense, especially when it came to men. You preach to us about passing up good men, and here you are with the phattest ring on your finger sittin' in *our* living room trippin' over a man that loves you. What you need to be doing is going to Michael's place saying 'yes Michael, I'll marry you even though I'm crazy as hell.'" LaShaun walked off to the kitchen.

"Tomiko, I could understand if you have reservations about marriage; and love; and relationships. Who wouldn't? Marriage *is* a big step. I just don't want you to pass up a good thing. Promise me you'll pray about this one. Don't let self-doubt rob you of the joy you deserve. Don't be blindsided by love, but don't be fooled by your own ideologies about love either."

"Yeah, don't be *no fool!*" LaShaun shouted from the kitchen where she beat eggs for an omelet, "because only a fool would give a ring back to a good man."

"This is not supposed to be happening to me. I wasn't always like this Cameron. I don't even know if I'm capable of loving someone the way a wife should love her husband. You all know the Tomiko from Brownsberry. I had another, completely different, life before I came to school. I don't think Michael would even want me if he knew all the things I've done before and it's just so hard to tell him I-" Tomiko was not ready to confess her past life to her friends. She did not want to conjure up the emotional baggage.

"Tell him you what?" Cameron consoled her. "Tomiko, you have to start trusting someone."

"Cameron, I'm not like you or LaShaun. I don't have the story of the good girl who made it out the hood. I'm the other girl in the story. I ran the blocks; I did things with people I don't want to retell. I'm not ready for this kind of relationship now. I'm going to tell Michael in a couple of days-I can't do it." Tomiko took in a deep breath, "but right now, I just need some time." She rose from the couch and walked towards the door.

"Tomiko," Cameron called after her, "you gotta know I'm here for you."

LaShaun hurried from the kitchen. "Are you leaving? I just started breakfast."

Tomiko shook her head declining the invitation. "Thanks Shaun, but I'm good." Tomiko walked out of the apartment, down the stairs of the breezeway and to her car. She opened the door and leaned on the top of the car catching her tears. *Damn Michael, I never even told him I loved him. Why would he propose to me? Why now?*

Chapter 11 the holiday spirits

Cameron waited outside the Oakland International Airport, hoping to see her mom and dad pull up in their silver Cadillac. She hated waiting at the airport for a ride. After four and a half hours of flying, standing around the airport was not her way of being welcomed home.

"Hey baby girl!" William, her father hollered out to her as he approached her.

Cameron turned around to see her dad, a short stocky man, dressed in a sharp wool hat and trench wool coat, coming out of the airport doors. She could always count on her father to be in style, at least for an old man. Her dad had a smile that made a little girl forget all her troubles, even if he arrived late.

"Daddy," she reached up and hugged her dad. His cologne warmed her nostrils with its fresh woody scent. "You smell good. Is that new cologne?"

"Something your mom bought me," her father shrugged his shoulders, attempting a role in modesty, a role he did not play well. "I don't know the name of it."

Cameron looked around for her mother to walk up behind him. "Where is mom?"

"I had to leave her. If I would've waited for her, I wouldn't have got here until midnight," her father complained. "You know how slow your mom is and she doesn't like to be rushed. Anyway, I gotta surprise for you. Come on." He grabbed Cameron's luggage.

Cameron joyfully followed her father through the parking lot. Being home reminded her she was the baby girl. It was her time to forget about being a responsible adult and she cherished her time with her family. Her dad walked towards a silver Mercedes Benz G500 and unlocked the doors.

"This is *your* car dad?" Cameron inquired about the unfamiliar car.

"Yep, this is it baby girl, surprise!" He waited to see the excitement on Cameron's face. Cars were their thing. Whenever he purchased something new, she drove it as if he brought it for her.

Cameron mumbled under her breath, "I can't believe I'm still catchin' the bus and you got a new Benz."

"Don't make me feel bad. You haven't asked me for any money, so if you're catchin' the bus, it's because you want to catch the bus. You know I'll give you anything you need. So don't start with me Cameron."

"Daddy, I know. I was just messin' with you." Cameron smiled in downplaying her financial constraints. She didn't like to bother her parents for money, because she did not want to become a burden to them. After all, they struggled to get her through her bachelor's degree. It had always seemed difficult for them to make ends meet when she was growing up. She learned to ignore her own needs so she wouldn't worry her parents. However, the Benz meant that somebody must have come into a new source of income.

Cameron's father opened the passenger side door for her. She climbed in and enjoyed the plush interior of the luxury vehicle and the smell of a new car. This was what Cameron wanted. How could her dad afford the luxury? Why were her parents still in the 'hood if her dad could afford a car that had to have cost him well over a hundred grand?

Cameron looked out the window and noticed how Oakland had changed so much since she'd left. Palm trees stood firmly from the ground as if they were natives of the land. She never remembered so many palm trees residing along 98th Avenue. Cameron felt like a foreigner in her hometown. She missed the developing city of Oakland. The ghettos were now areas of prime real estate, and everyone was trying to get their hands on the properties once noted for violent shootouts and turf wars.

"So, what's wrong with your car?"

Cameron sat with the palm of her hand supporting her chin, gazing out of the window. "My clutch went out."

"*Your clutch went out!*" Her father hollered like it was the last thing on earth that should have happened to her four-year-old car.

"Yes, dad, the clutch went out," Cameron retorted defensively. "You do know they don't last forever."

Recognizing the sarcasm in Cameron's voice her father playfully reached for her arm supporting her chin and swapped it.

Cameron's face jerked forward and she started laughing. "What?"

"Don't get smart with me, young lady." Her dad spoke as firmly as he could to his daughter. He was proud of her for finishing her bachelor's and pursuing a master's degree at a prestigious college.

"I'm not getting smart, I'm just sayin'-"

"I hear what you sayin', but this is your dad you're talking to not someone off the street."

"Whatever dad," Cameron waved her hand in the air, dismissing her father's comments.

After a moment's silence, her father continued his interrogation, "How much is it to get your car fixed?"

"Four-hundred-dollars."

"When were you going to tell somebody Cameron?"

Cameron cut him off, "I wasn't going to tell anyone. I wanted to get the money myself, but it's been over a month now and I don't know how I'm going to pay rent, all my other bills, and get my car fixed."

"Are you still working?"

"Dad, I'm in school. I can only work part-time right now and that's barely covering the bills."

They pulled into the driveway of her childhood home, a small three-bedroom home that reminded her of a small village abode. She knew her parents could probably get double what they paid, if they ever decided to sell it. Her dad put the car in park and looked at her, "Well, tell your mom before you leave so you can get that taken care of. There's no use in you having a car that you can't drive."

"Thanks dad," Cameron smiled and gave her father a hug, relieved she would be able to get her car back when she returned to Atlanta.

Katie, Cameron's mom, opened the door and stepped onto the porch when she heard the car pull into the driveway. Her mom's face glowed at the sight of her daughter returning home. Cameron looked twice at her mom. The highlighted gray and black tones of her mother's hair left Cameron with a question. When had her mother's hair gotten so gray? Although many things had stayed the same, so much changed since she left home for college. At that moment, Cameron realized her parents would not be here forever. It was not something she wanted to think about, but looking at her mom, she knew that something had been going on in the Turner household aside from her dad making extravagant purchases.

"Sis!" Her brother Octavius, also known as Big Tey, hollered as he jumped out of his 1963 champagne-colored Cutlass. Tey inherited his car fetish honestly and he kept his rides nice. Cameron wished he put as much into himself as he put into his possessions.

"What's up Tey?" Her brother had gained at least another thirty pounds since she had last seen him a year ago. She rubbed his belly and then gave him a hug, "What's all that? I guess you been eatin' good."

Tey laughed, "You know how I do sis."

"Hi mom," Cameron walked towards her mom who seemingly could not wipe the smile from her face.

"Oh baby, it's so good to see you." Her mom Katie held back tears and hugged her daughter. It had been hard for her to let Cameron leave when she first went away to college in Atlanta. Cameron was the youngest of their two children and their baby girl. Now that she was a grown woman, Cameron only saw her parents once a year. Airline tickets to California on a bi-yearly basis were much too expensive, especially now that she paid for her own tickets.

"Sis, you got plans for the night?"

"No, I'm taking it easy today." Cameron looked at her brother with suspicion, "Why? What's up?"

"We hangin' out at Friday's tonight. You want me to come pick you up?"

"Friday's?" Cameron wondered if that was a new club in Oakland.

"Yeah, Friday's at Jack London Square."

"Oh, they opened a Friday's at Jack London."

"Come on Cam, I know it hasn't been that long," Tey walked back to his ride, dragging his backside with him. "That Friday's been out there."

"Excuse me!" Cameron sarcastically replied,

"You know it's been a while since I've hung out in Oakland."

"You hella bootsie," Tey opened his car door. "I'll be back at eight."

Cameron laughed. She hadn't been called bootsie in a while. It was her brother's description of her for being out of touch with the latest happenings around town. That was her official welcome back home, and it was only eleven in the morning. She had plenty of time to freshen up and get ready for the evening.

"Come on inside baby, there's someone here that wants to see you." Her mom grabbed her by the shoulder, giving her a one armed hug.

Cameron hesitated going inside. She did not want to put on her polite hat so soon. Her mom always made her meet up with older friends that she could barely remember. Cameron walked in the door and noticed an attractive young man sitting on the couch. He wore a low cut hairstyle with light waves, and there was no noticeable hair on his smooth dark face.

"Raymond?" Cameron could not contain the excitement in her voice.

"Hey girl," Raymond replied, his baritone voice just as seductive as she remembered. He stood up claiming his six-foot-two inches of designated space and walked up to Cameron, wrapping his arms around her.

"What are you doing here? It's been forever since I've seen you." Cameron had a minor crush on Raymond when they were growing up. He moved out of the neighborhood after middle school and only occasionally stopped by to visit his grandparents.

"You know me, I just been staying out of trouble. Tryna' do my thang," Raymond primped himself, "Wow, you are lookin' good. What they feedin' ya'll in the south?"

"Shut up," Cameron blushed at the compliment and hit Raymond on his shoulder. "Did you know I was coming home today?"

"Yeah, I asked around about you. I always try to keep up with you." Raymond paused and allowed Cameron to catch his subtle flirtation. "In all seriousness, your brother told me you would be home today. You know I'm going to be comin' out to Atlanta soon. I got a scholarship to play basketball at Atlanta College."

"That is great! I am so excited for you. Well, you know I am down there. Just take my number and hit me up when you are in the area."

"Cool." Raymond paused, "So, what's up for the night?"

"I'm supposed to be hangin' out with big brotha tonight. You're more than welcome to tag along."

"Naw, I'll let ya'll do the family thing."

"Raymond, you are family." Cameron smiled and headed into the kitchen where she heard her mom telling her father off.

"I will do anything I goddamn please in my house." Katie yelled to her husband in the kitchen. "If I want to have another drink, you need to get me another drink!"

"Mom-Dad, is everything alright?" Cameron looked at her father, knowing things were never all right in the Turner household.

"Baby," Cameron's mom approached her with her arms open wide, "of course everything is alright."

Katie wrapped her arms around her daughter and placed Cameron's head in her bosom. Cameron could smell the holiday spirit on her mother's breath. Katie's holiday motto was 'deck the halls with lots of cognac.'

"Mom, you're drunk."

"Oh shit, here we go." Her mom walked to the kitchen window, which looked out towards the street.

Raymond suddenly appeared at the window.

"What the hell?" Katie hollered out, "You silly

fool. Why would you sneak up on somebody like that?"

"I just wanted to say bye moms." Raymond looked around Katie before she could make another snide remark, "Bye Pops. I'll talk to you later Cameron."

Cameron waved back quickly, embarrassed by her mom's foul tongue. "Mom, why are you drinking so much? It's too early in the afternoon for us to have to put up with this."

"Oh, so you gon' come all the way from Atlanta and tell me how to drink my muthafuckin' bottle? Yo' ass ain't been here in months. I know you not tryna' to tell me what to do. Please, you and yo' father could go somewhere. Ya'll don't have to put up with shit." Katie mumbled under her breath, lighting a cigarette, "I wish these niggas would try to tell me what to do in my house. I'm at home and I ain't botherin' nobody."

"Fine, I'm gone. I don't know why I come home anyway." Cameron stomped out of the kitchen.

"Look here, you little sassy wench. Don't you go runnin' out the door on me." Cameron stood completely silent against the front door of the home while her mom continued her rant. "Cameron, I said come here. Don't disrespect your mom. I birthed you little ass!"

"Katie, leave her alone." Her husband pleaded with her.

"Bill, shut the hell up." Katie pointed to her husband with a cigarette between her fingers. She called him Bill since high school as a nickname. "I'm that child's mother and she doesn't talk to me any damn way she wants. I gave the bitch life. You can let her talk to you like that, but I don't play that shit. I don't care what I'm doing. She needs to give me the respect I deserve." Turning away from her husband, Katie yelled out again, "Cameron, bring yo' ass back in here."

"What do you want?" Cameron yelled back.

"I said come here!"

Cameron slowly walked back into the kitchen,

"Yes mother."

"Now, what was that you were sayin'?"

"Nothing," Cameron sat against the kitchen wall, waiting for her mother to continue her traditional drunken lecture.

"Well, how was your trip?" Katie flashed between different personalities when she drank. Her mom's drinking was one of the reasons Cameron went across the country for school. She didn't want to be bothered with the dynamics of her family life while she studied in college.

"Mom, I really don't want to talk about this right now."

"Shit, fine by me," Katie put her cigarette back between her lips and started cleaning the collard greens she soaked in the sink with baking soda.

"Dad, I need to use your car. Can I borrow it for a few minutes?"

"Sure baby, just be careful next to the curbs. I don't want you messing up my tires." William handed her keys to his Benz.

Cameron had to get out the house. She headed towards 105th avenue to visit her cousins. This holiday would be as memorable as the ones in previous years, and all the ones to come if her mom kept drinking.

Chapter 12 time to move on

"Mom, it's a quarter after five already," Tomiko called upstairs to her mom. "Can we get there today?" Tardiness irritated her, especially when there was no good reason for it. Her mom knew how long it took to get ready. She could just start preparing for the event earlier rather than running late.

Tomiko paced from the window on the lower level of the Victorian style home to the bottom step. Traditionally, Tomiko and her mom would visit her grandmother for Christmas dinner. Since her grandmother passed, they never missed dinner at Nadine's, one of her mother's closest friends.

"Jeez Louise, I'm coming." Theresa walked down the stairs in a festive red shimmering sweater tank with a matching cardigan, an ankle length black skirt, and black boots. Her mom was a fashion plate, even in her late forties. "How do I look?" Tomiko watched her mom shift from side to side with her hands on her hips. She put her right foot back behind the heel of her left foot and spun around like a runway model. Her mom was five-feet-six-inches tall and had a beautiful honey complexion. The light from the foyer deflected from her mom's lustrous shoulder length hair that swayed back in place with ease. She remembered her mom's hair being very manageable, not too thick or thin, unlike Tomiko's fine hair.

Tomiko smiled, forgetting all about her agitation with being late. "You look great mom." Tomiko placed her mom's freshly pressed hair behind her shoulders with her fingers. "Now let's go."

"Do you have the wine?" Theresa asked as Tomiko grabbed the fur coat on the hook next to her mom's door and helped Theresa put it on. "Is the stove off? I better go check it."

"No mom, I got it." Tomiko softly pushed her mom towards the door that led to the garage assuring her she would double check everything in the house.

"Okay, stop rushin' me. I get all nervous and tense when you start rushing me."

Tomiko sassed her mom. "Whatever," She walked in front of her mom, disgusted with her nonchalant attitude about punctuality. "I'll be in the car."

"You do that!" Theresa insisted, "I just need a couple of more minutes and I'll be right behind you...and don't pull the car out the garage yet. It's not more convenient for me to walk through the front when the snow is piled up out there like that." Outside the snow built up on the sidewalks and the three-foot tall shrub bushes aligning the walkway of the two-story home.

Tomiko walked off, leaving her mom talking to herself, "Which reminds me, I need to call that boy and get him to shovel my driveway and walkway. Shoot, I hope Tomiko cleared that driveway." Theresa looked out the front window to see Marquis, her twelve-year-old neighbor, outside shoveling the drive. She grabbed her pocket book to look for five dollars. Smiling she ran to the door. "Marquis, here you go. Thank you so much how did you know I needed you today?"

"Tomiko called me yesterday to tell me you would need me Miss Bee. I'm sorry I was a little late, but I'm finished now."

"You're right on time." She handed him a five-dollar bill.

"Thank you ma'am, but Tomiko already paid me." He secretly enjoyed when Tomiko came in town, because she paid him double what Ms. Bordeaux paid.

"She did?" Theresa was taken aback by her daughter's gesture. She smiled at Marquis, "Well just take it anyway-Merry Christmas!"

"Thanks Miss Bee," Marquis grinned as if he had won the lottery.

"No problem sweetie. Tell your mom I said Merry Christmas." She reached back inside and picked up a box wrapped in red paper sitting by the side of the door, "Oh, and take her this."

"No problem Miss Bee." He took the red box from her and ran off waving, "and Merry Christmas to you."

Tomiko ran back in the house from the garage, "Mother, it's almost five thirty."

"I'm coming already."

This time, Tomiko sat by the door leading to the garage and waited for her mom with her arms folded. She watched over her mom as if their roles had changed. Theresa grabbed her purse, another small package from under the tree, and made her way to the car.

At last, they backed out of the driveway and Tomiko headed down the street to Nadine's house. She enjoyed going over Nadine's because she was like a second mother to her. Nadine could cook like her mom and grandmother. She was originally from New Orleans too.

"Well, baby, I'm glad you're home." Theresa patted her daughter's leg affectionately. "It just seems like you can never come home enough."

"I know mom. I'm trying to do better about seeing you more often. Besides, I wouldn't miss Nadine's Christmas dinner again for the world." Tomiko had rushed around the house all morning. She flew in at nine thirty that morning because she had to work late Christmas Eve. She would be back in Atlanta on Tuesday morning, which gave her three days to spend time with her family. Mr. Wallace would need the final report for Urban Gear once she was back at the office.

"Did you talk to Charlotte? She's been calling me since before you got here, wanting to know when you were going to make it. I told her you would be here this morning."

"No, I hadn't talked to her yet. Are you going with me later to take the gifts by her house?"

"No, I'll let you young folks hang out. You can leave me over Nadine's." Theresa looked at her daughter, her motherly instincts telling her that something was bothering Tomiko. "Is everything okay?"

Tomiko hesitated, "Mom, why won't you move to Atlanta with me?"

"Oh Tomiko," Theresa dismissed her daughter's suggestion. "I got a life out here; what would I do in Atlanta?" Theresa answered offensively.

"You know people out there."

"What about my shop, my friends, my house? That's just too much for me to do at this age."

"Mom, that's just an excuse. Plenty of people relocate at your age. The flower shop, that would take a little planning to relocate, especially since we don't have any family out here that we know could actually operate the shop, but didn't you say Nadine would be retiring in a year or so? Maybe we could hire her to be the store manager."

"I'm glad you said we, because I don't make enough to pay a manager."

"Mom, are you paying yourself a salary?"

"Of course I am. You wouldn't let me run the shop until I did."

"That could be Nadine's salary."

"Then what would I get paid?" Theresa managed her shop for years without Tomiko's input and she was upset her daughter tried to insinuate otherwise.

"You would make money off the profits as the owner." Tomiko explained logically, "that is the benefit of being an owner. You are not supposed to run the shop your whole life. You have to make a plan to sustain the business when you are gone. The business is your estate, unless you want it to dissolve. Is it just something to keep you busy until..."

"I don't want to talk about this. Why do you want me to move to Atlanta? I have everything I need right here in Chicago; everything except you."

"And a man," Tomiko interjected.

"A man," Theresa looked at Tomiko in shock. "Is that what you think I need, a man? Baby girl, I will have you to know that I am doing just fine." Theresa adjusted her sweater, pulling it in areas that seemed otherwise fine. "Are you afraid that I am lonely out here? Because I'm far from lonely. And don't you start trying to feel pity on me. I never took anyone's pity. This is the life I've created for myself and I'm proud of it. I have my own business, a car, a home. I don't ask or borrow from anyone, and I have a beautiful daughter that is intelligent and successful. And one of these days she should be giving me some grandbabies." Her mother chuckled.

Tomiko looked at her mother as if she had spoken a foreign language. "Don't hold your breath on that one."

"You're so worried about me getting a man.

You're young. I've had my fun but what about you? Where's your man?"

"Believe it or not, I'm engaged."

"Engaged!" Theresa shouted with pride in her voice. "Michael asked you to marry him? I always liked him."

"Mom, you haven't seen him since I was in college."

"Yes, but I liked him from the moment I met him. And he calls me all the time."

"He *calls* you?" This was news to Tomiko.

"I knew he was a good man when I first met him."

"Mom, how often do you talk to him?"

"Oh, it's no big deal." Theresa waved her hand, dismissing Tomiko's question. "He invited me to Atlanta a couple of times when he got worried about you. He's a really caring young man. And I know he loves you."

"So you think I should marry him?" There was an uncertainty in Tomiko's voice that her mother caught onto right away.

"What is wrong with him?"

"Nothing's wrong with him. I'm just not sure I'm ready for this type of relationship."

"There is nothing wrong with him, and there's nothing wrong with you."

Silence filled the car for the remainder of the ride. Tomiko loved her mom, but she feared Theresa would waste the rest of her life waiting on her dad to return to Chicago. It had been over twenty years since her mom last spoke to him. Her mother never explained the details of the relationship and she did not understand why her father disappeared out of their lives. She just prayed her mom would get enough nerve to leave the city and start a new life, because waiting on a man until she died would ruin her. Somehow, she sensed that if her mom could not be with the one she loved, she would be just fine if she never met another man at all.

"Great, we're here. Let's go." Theresa jumped out of the car as soon as Tomiko put the gear in park.

Tomiko and Theresa walked up to a house with cars lined up the driveway and down the street. Nadine knew how to throw a Christmas dinner party. It helped that a handful of her family lived in the city. Tomiko desperately wanted her mom to be close to family. Initially, that was her thought for her moving to Atlanta. Her grandmother died from an undiagnosed breast cancer seven years earlier, and her mom had been in Chicago by herself most of that time. All her family eventually moved back to New Orleans, including her only sister and two of her brothers. Tomiko's grandmother had property out there, and Theresa had allowed her brothers and sister to buy her out. She used the money to open her floral shop.

Tomiko couldn't wait to get around that table of gumbo, fried turkey, macaroni and cheese, candied yams, greens, potato salad and corn bread. When Tomiko opened the door, she saw a house filled with familiar faces. Her uncle had even made it up from New Orleans.

"Meeko," he ran up to her and grabbed her. Her uncle, Hank Junior, looked just as she remembered him. Even as an older man, Tomiko's uncle could be a model. He was tall, with a slender build and his naturally brown curly hair made him a hit with women. She wondered if he inspired her to achieve the look she had today. "Meeko, girl what you do with all your hair? I tell you, you and your cousin Stephanie are on the same thing. But you still my favorite niece. Come give your uncle a hug."

"Uncle Junior! Mom didn't tell me you were here. Where's my cousin?"

"She didn't want to do the family thing. She's visiting her fiancé's family." Her uncle said with a frown on his face.

"Stephanie is engaged?"

"...to some knucklehead boy. But I guess he's alright. Come on, let your uncle fix you something to drink." He grabbed her by her shoulders and turned to his sister, "Hey baby girl." He kissed Theresa on the cheek.

"Junior, don't you get my baby drunk now."

"She ain't no baby any more Reesa. I realized that when Stephanie came home with a ring on her finger."

Theresa shook her head in laughter and made her way to the kitchen where she knew Nadine would be putting the final touches on her desserts.

"You need help in here?" Theresa began to speak in her natural southern dialect.

"No, girl I'm good." Nadine looked behind her, "Where my girl at?" She asked with a deep Louisiana drawl.

"Her uncle out there tryna' get her drunk."

"Oh stop, that Junior is a mess." Nadine responded.

"I'm tellin' you. He ain't happy 'til everyone around him is drunk and on they face."

"He just want somethin' to laugh about in da' mornin' 'cause he know everybody can't handle dey liquor." Nadine interjected.

Nadine and Theresa laughed together.

Nadine and Theresa met in grammar school. They have been inseparable since the day Nadine ran off the girls in the fourth grade class with a four by four when they tried to jump on Theresa. She moved from Baton Rouge to New Orleans. She told Theresa, "You always gotta keep something on ya' wid dese girls 'round here. Dey ugly and mean." It was not something Theresa worried about until she got to New Orleans because all her family went to the same school in her hometown. No one ever messed with her in Baton

Rouge.

Theresa continued, "That crazy girl is tryna' get me to move to Atlanta."

"Now that would be a nice change for you."

"What does that mean?" Theresa was surprised to hear her friend agreeing with her daughter.

"I mean, you been in Chicago for years and you don't always seem happy 'til Meeko comes home, maybe being in Atlanta wid her will make you happy all da' time. Plus, you know I'll come visit you."

"She is the only person I could ever really depend on all my life. She's my baby." Theresa pondered on Tomiko's proposal to move to Atlanta.

"I understand that, so what's so wrong wid being wid yo' baby?"

"Hi Aunt Nadine!" Tomiko yelled from the kitchen entryway.

Nadine dropped her knife she'd been using to cut her key lime pie into slices and turned to greet Tomiko. "Here's my girl." Nadine had five boys, and it seemed as if her body was made of pure elastic; it always returned to her original shape. She had the figure of a twenty-one-year-old. Nadine wrapped her thin arms around Tomiko and rubbed her hair. "What you tryna' do up dere girl? You runnin' round here lookin like dem boys. Did you see Willie and nem? They been askin' 'bout you for a week now. Dey s'posed to be promotin' some party out here and dey want you to come."

"I just talked to them and Willie did mention something about me coming out to a party tonight."

"Are you going?" Her mom asked.

"I don't see me doing anything else tonight. I still can't get in contact with Charlotte."

"Just make sure that girl don't bring no weapons to the party." Nadine chuckled lightly, "She be lookin' like she going through it. Like she be ready to kill somebody. I be afraid to talk to her when I see her out."

"Nadine!" Theresa said forcefully, "Now that's not nice."

"She always been such a pretty girl. I don't understand why she would let herself go like dat."

"Auntie!" Tomiko looked at Nadine with disappointment, "now that girl ain't never done nothing to you."

"Well it look like somebody did a couple of things to her. Poor baby, after she had that lil' boy it just seem like she went crazy."

Theresa interrupted her, "Not everybody can handle being a single mother. It gets depressing sometimes."

"Well, if you were depressed I could never tell because you would never let yourself go like that." Nadine complimented Theresa.

"Is this what ya'll do when I'm not around?" Tomiko inquired, "Just gossip about everybody and what they are doing with their lives?"

Theresa looked at Nadine with a knowing glance. They laughed and answered at the same time, "Yeah."

Tomiko shook her head, as her cell phone began to ring.

"Is that Michael?" Theresa asked.

"Who's Michael?" Nadine inquired, "I know ya'll ain't left Aunt Nadine out of the loop."

"I gotta answer this…please excuse me." Tomiko walked out the kitchen, happy to be out the hot seat. "Girl, you got perfect timing."

"Merry Christmas trick!" LaShaun shouted over the phone.

"Merry Christmas Meeko," Cameron added.

"Ya'll hoes did not do a three way on me," Tomiko laughed. "Now I really feel like I'm in high school."

"How's the holiday going?" Cameron asked.

"I haven't exchanged gifts with my mom yet, but

we are over my Aunt Nadine's house and I'm about to tear me up some food. How's everything in Cali and Alabama?"

"Well you know out here on the West side, the sun is shining. It's sixty two degrees, daddy's on the grill smokin' a turkey and moms is drunk as a skunk, like always."

"Oh, you make me sick. It's freezing cold in Chicago."

Cameron sang and laughed, "I wish they all could be California girls."

"Whatever! Don't nobody want a Cali girl when they could have a Southern belle, because we know how to treat our men." LaShaun teased Cameron.

"That's right. I gotta represent N'Awlins on that one." Tomiko replied.

Cameron dismissed both comments, "Anyway, what's the haps? We are trying to figure out if we should be makin' it back to Atlanta for New Year's Eve."

"Unfortunately, I have to be back to work by Wednesday, so I'll be leaving Chicago Tuesday," Tomiko replied regrettably.

"I'm only three hours away, so it is really up to ya'll." LaShaun responded.

"Okay, that is cool with me. I don't think I can take another day of arguing with my mom about her being drunk. I sure didn't come home for this."

"You know nothing changes at home. We just leave all the problems here, but they're still here when we get back." LaShaun encouraged Cameron, "But that's why we left, to make it better for the future."

"You ain't neva lied." Cameron laughed and agreed.

"Well, I guess it's final. I'll come home on the twenty-ninth. Cameron, did you send the check off for the electric bill?" LaShaun asked.

"Yes, what do you think I'm irresponsible?"

Cameron replied sarcastically.

"Just askin', don't get your panties all in a bunch."

"Well, I'll talk to ya'll later, I am slightly at a party." Tomiko checked around the room and saw Nadine's son Willie approaching her.

"Excuse us! We'll holla at you later." LaShaun replied. "Bye Cameron."

"Peace."

Chapter 13 road to recovery

"Who was that?" LaShaun's mom sashayed into her bedroom, wearing an orange and bright green muumuu. The tail end of the hair comb stuck out of her hair holding the side of her hair down, while the other wore the adornments of an assorted color of plastic rollers.

LaShaun could see her grandmother in her mom more and more as the years passed. Her hips were narrow and her chest rested in her lap whenever she sat down. Her mother was short in stature, at five-foot four inches tall. LaShaun had grown a couple of inches taller than her.

"That was my business." LaShaun rolled to her stomach, to reach across her bed and hang up the phone receiver on its base. She checked her cell phone menu to see if she had missed any calls during her short nap.

"Okay, your business on my phone." Sabrina turned to leave the room.

"I'm just playin' mom." LaShaun had often amused herself by making her mom get an attitude. "It was Cameron and Tomiko. We were trying to decide where we are going for New Year's."

"Oh I see, and what do you ladies have planned for New Year's Day?" Sabrina asked in a prim and proper manner. She walked back towards the bed her daughter comfortably claimed every holiday season. After all, it was her childhood bedroom.

LaShaun snatched a pillow from the headboard and placed it under her chin, "Nothing right now, just the fact that we are all going to be in the same city." LaShaun looked at her mom, wondering how she was doing because her mom always seemed together even when turmoil was around her. Their family dynamics had continued to change since they discovered drug paraphernalia in the home. "Hey, are you alright?" She asked in concern.

"I guess I'll be alright. Dinner is almost finished but we are heading out to your grandmother's in the next hour or so." No matter where LaShaun's family went for the holidays, her mom always made a meal they could come back to at home.

"With yo' head lookin' like that?"

LaShaun's mom picked up a pillow and threw it at her daughter. "Silly girl, I'm hot combing it and curling it as I go."

"Oh, because I was gettin' ready to say-" LaShaun could not hold back the tears from laughter when she imagined her mom walking out the house with her hair half combed.

"You were gettin' ready to say what?" Her mother engaged her.

"You look like your husband's wife now." LaShaun laughed aloud.

"That's not funny LaShaun." Her mom's seriousness wore on her face when it came to her husband and his issues that seemed to ripple through the family. LaShaun and her two brothers found out about their father's drug habit two years earlier, after her brother Arnold Junior, or A.J. as they called him, hooked up with some of the other boys in the neighborhood and started selling drugs.

"Well if you can't laugh about it, you'll be miserable for the rest of your life." LaShaun reminisced over the disorder her family had gone through after the discovery. She never looked at her dad with the same respect and admiration that she had for him when she was growing up.

"Did you talk to your baby brother yet?" Sabrina asked, taking a seat on the edge of the bed.

"About what?" LaShaun knew if her mom asked about talking to her younger brother, Terrance, something was going on with him, and usually he was in some kind of trouble.

"He got some girl pregnant. So he's about to be a father at sixteen." Sabrina held her head down, attempting to restrain tears.

"Mom, it's okay. Please don't start crying." LaShaun wiped her mother's eyes.

"I rarely see your brothers anymore. They come and go outta here like it's no tomorrow." She sighed and took in a deep breath, "I know finding out your dad was on drugs upset them. Ever since then, the two of them have just gotten out of control. Your dad can't say anything to them, and I might as well be invisible."

"You mean Arnold's been actin' up too? I thought he was takin' classes at the community college."

"He's takin' classes and hangin' out with the wrong crowd at the same time. I swear these kids don't know what's good for them. And he's s'posed to be the oldest child. He doesn't have any idea what he's doing to himself by hangin' out with them boys, smokin' weed and drinkin'. I'm so frustrated LaShaun. I'm so frustrated. It seems like since you've been gone, everything is getting worse.

"And your father, if he ain't high, he don't say nuthin'. Then he does all that talkin' when nobody wanna be bothered with him."

"Mom, go get dressed and don't stress out about it. Dad has to make up his mind if he wants to kick his habit and get some help."

"I feel like it's my fault."

"It's not your fault mom." LaShaun sat by her mother's side attempting to comfort her. "You're not the one on drugs." She stood and helped her mother up. "Come on, finish getting dressed. I'll drive to Grandma's."

Sabrina raised herself slowly from LaShaun's bed and smiled at her daughter. "I'm so happy you're home." She hugged her daughter.

"Oh gosh, please mom." LaShaun knew her mom was being sentimental and she wasn't strong enough to keep herself together for that. "I love you too." She pulled away from her mother and headed to the bathroom before her mother's emotional wind gusted her way.

"Terrance," Sabrina called out to her youngest child. "Terrance, get up and start getting ready." He and LaShaun's bedrooms were adjacent to each other.

Terrance did not respond back. Sabrina walked into his bedroom. He sat propped up on his bed, headphones on, with a notepad and pen in his hands. Terrance looked just like his father at sixteen, slim build, dark brown skin and soft black curls in his hair. When he stood up, he reached six feet and two inches.

"Terrance," his mother called out to him. He continued to nod his head and write in his notepad. She walked over to him and he jerked his attention from his writing and attended to his mom.

"Mom, what's up?" He smiled at her and slid the headphones off his ears. He rested them around his neck.

"Are you finished getting dressed? We are about to go to your grandmother's." She stood over him with her hands on her hips.

"Is dude going?" He asked with a disappointed look on his face.

"Who is 'dude'? Are you referring to your father?" His mother put her hand across her chest to bear the insult and lack of respect he had for his parents.

"Mom, you know who dude is. I'm not riding nowhere with a dope fiend."

"Terrance, that's enough. He is still your father."

"He ain't none of my pops." He shook his head and put his headphones back on top of his head.

LaShaun walked in on her younger brother's conversation with his mom, irritated with his obstinate and disrespectful behavior, "Terrance, turn that headset off."

He turned off his radio and slid the headphones back off. "Man, ya'll buggin'. I'm tryin' to write my rhyme. I'm not bothering anyone and that's all I want to do right now. I don't need a lecture Shaun."

"Good, because I'm not going to give you one. First of all, you're not only disrespecting dad, you're disrespecting mom by not doing what she asks you to do. So put your shoes on and let's get ready to go. We don't have all day and you know how grandma is about us gettin' to dinner late."

"Man!" Terrance got up from his bed, smacking his lips and mumbling under his breath. He walked to his closet rummaging through his shoes.

"Ya'll don't make Arnold do nuthin'. Why I get treated like a little kid?"

"Cause you are a little kid." LaShaun yelled back.

"*What I do*?" Terrance wailed out.

"Lose the attitude," LaShaun snapped back at him. A thumping noise penetrated the walls of the house. The bass from a car's speakers made the windows of the home shake. LaShaun remembered a time when she would run to the window just to see who was passing by the house. The loud noise bothered her now that she was an adult. "Who is that?" LaShaun asked, annoyed by the rattling of the glass windows from the vibrations of the music's bass.

"That's my brother." Terrance ran out of the room to the front door as Arnold pulled up the driveway in his 1980 Chevy Caprice with a new aero descent paint job. "What's up A.J.? What you gettin' into today?"

Arnold walked up the steps of his childhood home and greeted his brother with a handshake and hug. He wore a brown and orange designer sweater with matching jeans. His silver chain hung below his chest and he wore a watch that looked similar to a Rolex. It glimmered in the winter sunlight. Arnold didn't live at home any longer, but he came home at least twice a week to visit his family. "Man, moms called me and told me we was goin' to Grandma's and shit for dinner. I know you didn't think I was missin' Grandma's Christmas dinner."

"Who is that in the car with you?" Terrance scoped his brother's ride.

"Shelly, she's a college freak I've been dating. But she's cool though."

"It gotta be more than that big bruh. You bringin' her home to meet moms."

`"Moms met Shelly a while ago. You just ain't been home to meet her. How's yo' girl?"

"I don't know how many times I'm gon' tell ya'll. That is not my baby."

"Shit if it ain't. Where's moms and lil' sis?" Arnold walked into the house, passing his little brother and walking towards the bedrooms.

"They're inside." Terrance followed behind his brother. "I can roll with you then?"

"Nigga, how you gon' ask me some stupid shit

like that." Arnold looked back giving his brother a
disappointed look. "Of course you can roll with me. You
think I would dis my family over some broad? You
know me better than any nigga out here, you should
know me better than that."

The door leading to the basement opened before
Arnold and Terrance walked to the back rooms. Arnold
Senior stood face to face with his two sons, a moment
that had rarely happened over the past few years.

"What's up pops? Merry Christmas!" Arnold
greeted his father the same way he did his brother
minutes earlier.

"Hey A.J.!" His father always got excited when
his boy came home. "Merry Christmas man. You coming
with us to dinner?"

Arnold looked at his younger brother and shook
his head, "Why ya'll keep askin' me these crazy
questions like I don't be with my family? It's the
holidays." He retreated to the back of the house,
throwing his hands in the air. "Of course I'm going to
my grandmother's for dinner. Where's my mom and my
sister? Ya'll crazy."

LaShaun helped her mother take the rollers out of
her hair and curled the remainder of it.

"A.J.," she shouted at the sight of her brother's
reflection in the bathroom mirror. She dropped the hot
curlers on the bathroom counter top. Two days had
passed since she arrived in Birmingham, and she was
happy to see her older brother. Her mother sat in the
mirror, smiling at the reunion. Arnold kissed his mother
on the cheek as she picked up the hot curlers to begin
where LaShaun left off.

"Hey mom, Merry Christmas," Arnold kissed his
mom while reaching in his pocket. He pulled out a small
box wrapped in green shimmery Christmas paper and
handed it to her. "This is for you."

"Thank you Arnold."

"Where's mine?" LaShaun jokingly asked.

"I got you next time lil' sis," Arnold loudly clapped both of his hands together, creating an echo throughout the house. "So, how's it goin' down? I'm ready. Terrance said he's riding with me, and I told you I was bringin' Shelly. She's in the car waitin' on me."

"Why didn't she come in?"Sabrina asked, offended by the lack of etiquette on the part of her son's friend.

"Who is Shelly?" LaShaun inquired.

"Shelly-" Arnold paused and turned the question to his mother. "Mom, explain to her who Shelly is."

"I wanna know why she didn't come in to speak to me." Sabrina continued.

"Mom, come on, don't trip on me. I'm 'bout to go. I thought ya'll would be ready so I told her to hang out in the car 'cause I'm not goin' to Grandma's late this year." Arnold walked out the bathroom.

"If you rollin' with me, let's go!" He hollered through the house.

LaShaun sat in the bathroom watching her mom curl her hair. "That boy is a mess mom."

"I know." Sabrina dropped the curlers and styled her hair with a wide toothcomb. She applied a light shimmering gloss to her lips. "Okay, I'm ready."

"Yes you are." LaShaun grabbed her purse and keys from the bedroom, and drove her mom and dad to the family meeting place. No matter what was going on in the family, nothing beat being with everyone during the holidays. LaShaun knew that her family had issues, but if you looked in everyone's heart, they all loved each other. Terrance was going through growing pains and he would eventually come around to forgive his father, just as Arnold had seemed to do. As far as she was concerned, family issues in Birmingham would remain in Birmingham. She had enough to deal with when she got back to Atlanta without worrying about her family.

Chapter 14 ditching the girls

"Burn that scented candle!
This is for all my people livin' life with regrets
Mad 'cause you live paycheck to paycheck.
Hell, at least you gotta job,
And I'm not tryin' to come off as some type of snob,
But it's time for a reality check.
It's time to stop procrastinatin' and sayin' what the heck.
I didn't come to hitcha with a deep poem and big words,
I just came because there is a message to be heard.
The average human only uses ten percent of their brain.
Only, ten percent of their brain, so I guess the other
ninety percent is trained to,
Go in from nine to five; walk the dog; watch the tube;
And let you sleep on, what you really can do.
Burn that scented candle!
Because that candle represents all the things you won't
do.
And all the things that you have the potential to be

But you're so afraid to light that candle and set that aroma free.

I'm tired-I'm tired of not living out my true destiny,
So I burned my scented candle!

And just as that candle has a purpose to keep a pleasant scent in this place,

I too have a purpose, I'm more than just skin taking up space.

And for those of you who don't know what that candle really means;

It means that for this New Year it's time to come clean.

It's time to stop talkin' about it and start livin' out those dreams.

It's time to write up the plan for that big money scheme.

It's time to start using that other ninety percent.

It's time to stop takin' jobs just to pay rent.

And it's time to start readin' that Bible a little more each day,

Because the time is coming when you'll need a word,

And John 3:16 shouldn't be the only scripture you can say.

You're going to need Jeremiah 29:11 to know that God has plans for you,

And you might need Psalm 118:8 to know that only He will get you through.

Burn that scented candle!

When you burn it,

It's going to physically change,

And just as that candle is changing your mentality will change too.

Because that's what it's supposed to do

And that's what He intended for you

And no I'm not a walking model of what a Christian should do, but you betta..."

The crowd helped Cameron finish the latter part of the poem, "Burn that scented candle!"

Cameron's poem addressed a second person, but she had written it to encourage herself during her stay in California.

Yusef took the stage proudly, "Cameron the Chameleon ya'll. Fiyah! Don't touch her, ya' might get burned. No pun intended. I have an announcement to make. Do you ever feel like you're in a Baptist church when you're here? Someone is always making an announcement." Yusef laughed at himself, "Anyway, WPWR is hosting an open mic event, scheduled at the 14th Street Playhouse on March seventh. There is limited space on the list and it will be on a first come first serve basis. The show will start at 8:00 p.m. and they expect all performers to arrive no later than 7:30p.m."

"Cameron, we are about to bounce girl. This is not how I imagined spending my New Year's Eve." Tomiko looked around, "I wanted to be shaking my booty at midnight, not burning a scented candle."

LaShaun and Tomiko laughed.

"Tomiko, I asked you what you wanted to do. No one made a suggestion and no one had a counter to the Poetry Lounge's New Year party. What's the big deal?"

"The big deal is, there are no fine men here — not even your friend Gordon. I'm going home."

"But you're engaged. You don't need to be lookin' for no fine guys." LaShaun reminded Tomiko.

"Physically I'm engaged, not mentally."

"Well it's too late to join a party now. It's almost midnight." Cameron argued with Tomiko. "Anyway, I don't have all that money to pay for a club on New Year's Eve. The least you're going to pay is a fifty dollar cover."

"Well, this is cool, but I need to find a party." Tomiko pressed her back against her seat and crossed her arms.

"Yeah Cam, I'm with Meeko. This ain't no type of party."

Cameron menacingly stared at LaShaun.

"But it's cool," LaShaun backtracked. Suddenly, her phone vibrated against her hip. "Excuse me for a minute."

"Booty call!" Tomiko teased as LaShaun grabbed her phone from her pocket.

"You all in my business." LaShaun made her way to the bathroom. There was no way to be discreet around Tomiko. "What's up?"

"Where you at?" Jason asked without any salutation.

"I'm up here at this Poetry party."

"*Poetry*? That shit is for lames. When are you leaving?"

"I don't know. Cameron drove up here and she is not ready to go."

"I'll come pick you up. Tell me where you are."

"I'm not sure about that one. You know us girls. We come together and we leave together."

"Are you a child or an adult? You'll be sleeping alone like Cameron tonight. You betta leave 'Us Girls' alone and roll with some testosterone."

"You are so romantic."

"Yeah, and you like it."

"I tell you what," LaShaun apprised him of her plans. "Let me call you back in fifteen minutes. We should be on our way out the door by then."

"Cool, just holla at a playa."

"Alright, I'll call you later." LaShaun hung up her cell phone and stuck it in her pocket. She walked out of the bathroom door, trying to conjure up an excuse to escape from her two girlfriends to meet up with Jason. She anticipated the snide remarks from Tomiko, and the disappointed look on Cameron's face when she excused herself for the evening. As LaShaun made her way through the crowd of poetic fans, she bumped into a man whose cologne reached her nostrils before he did.

"Oh, excuse me."She lightly leaned on his forearm for balance.

When the man recognized her, he called out to her in surprise. "*LaShaun?*" the familiar man asked.

"*Corey?* What in the world are you doing here?" LaShaun smiled and gave him a hug, "What's up with you man?"

"Shit, nuthin'." He sipped on a bottle of Heineken.

"I like your fit." Corey wore a replica of Magic Johnson's Lakers jersey, baggy denim jeans, and purple, gold and white Converse that matched the jersey.

"You know how a brotha does it." Corey popped the collar of the white t-shirt he wore under his jersey and released his magnetic smile in the dimmed venue.

"Who are you here with? How long have you been here?" LaShaun looked over Corey's shoulder for a familiar face.

"I'm here with Dre," Corey laughed as he joked with LaShaun.

"Very funny," LaShaun rolled her eyes to assure Corey she did not find his comment amusing. LaShaun's relationship to Corey preceded that of Andre's. She had met Corey as part of a traditional relationship builder between Brownsberry and Mooresmill College, another Historically Black College and University in the same city. She and Corey were sister and brother through an adopted family program.

"My bad," Corey continued to laugh and sipped his beer. "But uhm, where's your girl? I know she's not too far."

"Actually, she's right at the table over there." LaShaun pointed over many heads into a plethora of candlelit tables. It would have taken a hawk's eye to identify a familiar face in the crowd from Corey's location.

"Show me." Corey prompted LaShaun to lead

him by placing his hand in the small of her back. They made their way through the crowded bar where most people were hanging around just to socialize.

LaShaun and Corey reached the table where Cameron and Tomiko sat listening to the poet on stage.

Tomiko looked up and noticed Corey standing right beside LaShaun. She commented under her breath to Cameron, "Oh shit, look what the cat dragged in." Cameron looked over her shoulder to see Corey behind her.

"What's up girl?" Corey nudged Cameron with his forearm.

Cameron smiled excited to see him again; more than she anticipated or showed. "What's up?"

He stood with his left hand in his pocket, Heineken in his other hand and smiled.

"Come holla at me for a minute." He motioned for Cameron to follow him with a gentle nod of his head.

"Excuse me?" Cameron turned to him, blushing in her failed attempt to dismiss his demand for her company.

Corey pulled her seat back to give her room to step away from the table. "Man, come here." Corey insisted, and walked away confident she would follow him.

"Don't look at me like you are waiting for my approval or something. Go on and run off with yo' man." Tomiko responded to Cameron's silent question.

"He's not my man." Cameron smiled and threw a napkin at Tomiko, "At least, not yet."

LaShaun sat down at the table, reassured that Cameron would not care what she did with the rest of her night. Now she had to deal with Tomiko by herself.

"Why are you staring at me?" LaShaun asked defensively.

"This Corey thing is all your fault. I don't even want to hear about Corey this time around." Tomiko responded.

LaShaun fanned her hand at Tomiko. "Cameron is a grown woman. If she wants to date that man, she can and I'm a grown woman too so I'm about to blow this joint."

"Uhn-uhn, where are you going?"

"To mind my business. Tell Cameron I will see her at the house."

"So what am I supposed to do?" Tomiko pouted.

"I don't know, but if I were you, I would call my fiancé." LaShaun grabbed her purse and slid out of her chair.

"I'm not calling him because then he's gon' want some, and I don't have anything to give him."

"Tomiko, why are you playin'? You and I both know you gon' give that man some before the year is out."

"Thanks Peter," Tomiko snapped at LaShaun in reference to the Biblical disciple's ambivalent faith. "Ye of so little faith."

"I'm just sayin' get it over with already. Make that man happy. He's making you happy whether you want to admit or not." LaShaun threw two fingers in the air and gave Tomiko the peace sign. "See ya'."

Cameron walked back to the table with a drink in her hand.

"Where's mine?" Tomiko asked, disdained by her friends' ability to continue the party without her.

"I thought you weren't drinking anymore and I didn't want to encourage you." Cameron sipped on the glass of wine.

"Dammit," Tomiko hit her hand against the table. "I need two shots to deal with tonight's activity. Ya'll got too much goin' on."

Cameron laughed, "Tomiko, calm down."

"I'm ready to go."

"Fine, you know what? Let's just go! I'm tired of

arguing with you about why we are here." Cameron started to put on her coat and looked around after noticing a player was missing, "Where is LaShaun?"

"The heifa left." Tomiko picked up her purse, "And I'm ready to get out of here too."

"Well who did she leave with?"

"Am I my sister's keeper? I don't know where she went. She wouldn't say but more than likely it was Jason. Oh and by the way she said, 'don't wait up for her. She's a grown woman and she'll see you at the house.'"

"I'm sure something got lost in translation there."

"You want the watered down version, or you want me to get to the point; because all that was said in between is irrelevant."

"I wouldn't expect anything less from you Tomiko." Cameron slipped her coat and gloves on.

"Are you going to say good night to Corey?" Tomiko teased her friend.

"I already did. Let's go." Cameron lightly grabbed Tomiko's arm to lead her to the exit.

"Can I grab my coat?" She jerked her arm from Cameron's grasp, "Why are you in such a hurry now?"

"Let's go." Cameron didn't want to deal with the dichotomous personality of her friend. She wanted to leave the party on a high note, excited about what the New Year would bring for her and Corey.

"Yeah, you rushin' me because you hidin' something, but you best believe I know everything. Even the things you don't tell." Tomiko removed her coat from the chair one shoulder at a time, while Cameron impatiently watched Tomiko's movements. "You're going to have sex with him."

"*What*?" Cameron asked, offended.

"I know what that huffy breath means. It means a virgin is about to get laid."

"Can we go before you embarrass me?" Cameron

left her at the table.

The cold weather greeted Cameron when she walked out the door. She tucked her hands firmly in the pockets of her dress length wool coat, covered her chin with her scarf and placed her chin down. Cameron had an answer for this year's winter.

"Cameron wait up! I know you're not mad. That is something that you share with your friends."

"Well, I don't know what I'm going to do right now." Cameron stopped in the middle of the parking lot and faced Tomiko. A black Escalade whisked passed them. Tomiko identified LaShaun riding in the passenger side of the truck.

"It was Jason," Tomiko said glaring into the taillights of vehicle.

"What?" Cameron asked with an ambiguous look on her face.

"LaShaun just left with Jason." Tomiko pointed, but the Escalade cleared her line of sight before Cameron saw it. "All I'm sayin' is don't go throwin' it at the first man that asks."

Cameron laughed and shook her head. She walked towards her car and unlocked the doors. She had been so happy to come back home with the money to get it rolling, thanks to her dad.

"What's funny?"

"You think Corey is the first man that ever approached me about having sex?" Cameron shook her head again, "You really don't know me."

"I know men have invited you from the club, but not someone that you really like, like Corey. I just don't want you to get hurt the first time. It's supposed to be special."

They both sat in the car, allowing the defrost system to work on her windows. "Well, I used to want it to be special, but now I just want it over with. I just want to lose it." Cameron removed her hands from the gloves and tried to warm them near the vents of the car.

"You act like it's a curse. Girl, virginity is a gift. I hate I have to start all over with it." Tomiko attempted to encourage her.

"Yeah but it's different for you because you've experienced it already. I haven't. I want to know what it feels like."

"It's not all that, believe me. Why do you think I'm trying to get it back now? I'm just thankful I can be born again."

"That's easy to say after you've done it a thousand times."

"Oh, what are you *trying* to say?" Tomiko squared her shoulders to Cameron.

"No, I'm just sayin'." Cameron thought cautiously about the next statement. Sometimes Tomiko acted sensitive about the number of men she slept with, but other times she was a self-proclaimed slut. "Never mind, it doesn't matter."

"Don't think you're any better than me because you're a virgin. Everybody got they somethin' and mines just happens to have a dick."

"Tomiko, please don't get offended. I wasn't trying to call you out."

"You know what? Dick ain't such a bad thing. I'm tired of everyone acting like sex is just the evilest of all sins. If it was so dirty, God wouldn't have created it."

"Tomiko-" Cameron tried to interrupt her humbly.

"You know what, just take me home." Tomiko folded her arms across her chest and stared out the passenger side window.

"I'm sorry," Cameron apologetically whispered as she pulled the car out of the parking space.

"Me too," Tomiko set her focus on the darkness of the night and refused to look at Cameron. Cameron could barely take the silence on the way to Tomiko's downtown condominium.

"Tomiko, you know you're my girl, right?" Cameron continued to engage her in light conversation. "We didn't even stick around for the countdown tonight."

Nothing averted Tomiko's attention to whatever star she seemed to capture in the sky. Cameron realized the damage a few words could do to a friendship and she remembered how the tongue is sharp, piercing and cuts. Cameron pulled in front of Tomiko's high-rise building off Peachtree Street.

"Bye Meeko." Cameron tried once again to reach out to her friend before the night ended.

"Bye." The wind from the door slam bit Cameron in the face. She watched Tomiko walk up the stairs to her place, just as she did on other nights when they went out. This time, watching Tomiko and saying goodbye seemed a bit permanent. They never fell out. The situation was quite uncomfortable for Cameron and she prayed for a way to fix it. Tonight, she would let Tomiko sleep it off and maybe she would be more amiable in the morning.

LaShaun turned up the seat warmer on the passenger side of the truck, leaned her head against the soft leather headrest, and stretched her back in the body of the seat. She let the feeling of comfort consume her.

"You look good tonight. What is that you got on over there?" Jason peeked at LaShaun through the corner of his eyes.

"This old thing," LaShaun pulled her sequenced black tube shirt up higher on her chest and moved her legs, one crossed over the other to show off her black sandals.

"Good Lord! How do you wear sandals in the middle of winter?"

"It's fashionable," LaShaun responded with

confidence.

"I bet it won't be fashionable for one of those toes to fall off from frostbite."

"Jason, shut up." LaShaun closed her eyes and tried to put herself back into a meditative state.

LaShaun noticed Jason wasn't getting on the freeway, the normal route to her house. "Where are we going?"

"I gotta surprise for you."

"I love surprises!" LaShaun unsnapped the straps of her sandals that were cutting the circulation in her feet. Fashionable or not, her feet felt tenderized. If her skin tone was a hue lighter, her feet would have resembled the inside of a rare sirloin steak.

Jason pulled his Escalade into the valet parking driveway at The River, a jazz restaurant in downtown Atlanta. Once inside the slightly lit restaurant, the host escorted them to a table near the stage. A couple of band members were tuning their instruments before the next set.

The waitress walked over to the table with two glasses of water in her hand. She placed a glass of ice water in front of LaShaun and the other in front of Jason. She pulled her ordering pad from her black apron and greeted them. "Hi, my name is Tina. I will be your server for tonight."

"Happy New Year Tina," Jason sat up, mimicking the server's perkiness.

LaShaun noticed Tina's composure change from the insult of Jason's childish antics. She held her head down with her index finger on her temple while Tina continued to speak.

"Happy new year to you too," Tina smirked back at Jason. "The special of the night is salmon in a white wine sauce and if you want a little luck in your life for the New Year, we are also serving black eyed peas with brown rice as a side selection just for tonight. I'll give you a minute to look over the menu. Would you like to put in a drink order?"

"We'll take a bottle of Merlot."

Tina nodded and began to walk off.

"*Merlot*?" LaShaun questioned him loudly causing their server to slow her stride.

Jason raised his hand to signal Tina's departure. "Yes, Merlot. It's a red wine and it's good for you."

"Jason, I don't even like wine, especially red wine."

"It's okay. I'm here to expose you to the finer things in life girl. You can thank me later. What did you want to eat?" He rubbed the side of her arm as if his response comforted her.

"I guess whatever you will be ordering for me." LaShaun unraveled her silverware from her napkin to keep her composure in the restaurant.

"Great, we'll have the lamb with mint sauce."

LaShaun smiled and sipped her water. She never ate lamb and the pork chops were definitely more appealing to her.

"How did you get this table? You didn't tell me we had plans tonight." LaShaun tried to show that she was appreciative of Jason's inept attempt at thoughtfulness. After all, she could still be sitting in the poetry spot with Tomiko and Cameron, coming up with ways to get home. LaShaun knew it was no easy task to get reservations anywhere on New Year's Eve in Atlanta without paying an attractive fee.

"You ask a lot of questions." Jason did not answer directly.

"I'm just curious. I know you must have had to do a lot to get this table, especially right by the stage. This is a prime location."

"Well, you know. I do what I do. Speaking of, my boy is getting me tickets to the Young-T album release party. You wanna come with me?"

"Oh, yeah, your friend that manages him?"

"Yeah, that joker owes me a favor. The party isn't for a few weeks but I figured I would give you heads up."

LaShaun smiled. She would soon reap the benefits of being patient with Jason. He was already committing to a future date with her. It was a milestone towards the progression of their relationship.

Tina arrived with a bottle of Merlot, expertly popped the corkscrew out of the bottle and poured two glasses of wine. Jason ordered dinner. "I'm going to take the prime rib, medium well with a baked potato and she's having the lamb with mint sauce."

"Great choices," Tina nodded. "Are you going to have a side with the lamb?" She looked at LaShaun.

Before she could answer, Jason butted in, "She'll have a side salad with ranch dressing…light ranch dressing."

LaShaun smiled sheepishly. She would give Jason the opportunity to take the lead in the relationship. After all, it was what she wanted from him. She convinced herself to be receptive to new experiences with Jason. She began with the glass of wine sitting in front of her. She put the wine to her mouth and held her breath. The smell alone discouraged her from enjoying it. She took a small swig. Dry wood was the only thing she could think of while swallowing the wine. Who would want to drink liquid dry wood?

Jason picked up his glass of wine, and tilted it in simulation of a toast, "See, it's not so bad after all."

LaShaun let the wine trickle slowly down her throat like bad medicine, while nodding her head in feigned agreement with Jason. She finished the sip with a hard swallow. "Not so bad after all."

"Happy New Year baby," Jason lifted his glass to LaShaun, leaned across the table and kissed her as the entire restaurant began counting down.

"5-4-3-2-1, Happy New Year!" the crowd shouted.

Chapter 15 a new beginning

Cameron stood outside the familiar college park townhome, contemplating whether she should ring the doorbell. What was she doing at this man's home?

Her cell phone rang and she fumbled to retrieve it from her purse. Corey's number appeared on the screen. A confirmation she was exactly where she needed to be tonight. Cameron ignored the ringing phone and pressed the doorbell. She waited for Corey to answer.

He opened the door with a black cordless phone near his ear. He smiled and admitted, "I was just leaving you a message."

Cameron blushed and shyly walked past him. "I'm here."

"You sure are." Corey smiled, admiring her from a distance.

Cameron took off her winter protective gear and placed it on the couch. Corey came up behind her to pick up her coat. He tucked her gloves in the coat pocket and hung it neatly in his closet near the front door.

"Did you eat?" He asked her.

Cameron remembered he was a great cook. "As a matter of fact, I didn't. What did you cook?"

"I just made some gumbo. You wanna try it?"

"Sure, I wanna try it."

"Come on." Corey smiled at her and led her to his kitchen. She followed him. Corey had a half-finished bottle of Hennessey on the table.

"I see you saved me some Hennessey." Cameron picked up the bottle and teased Corey.

Corey poured a cup of Hennessey for himself, "Want some?" He tipped the bottle in Cameron's direction.

"No, I'm not a big 'Hen' drinker."

Corey prepared a bowl of gumbo and rice for Cameron. She could see the crab legs poking up from the big pot. The smell of seafood gumbo was a mouth-watering stimulant for Cameron. She pulled up a stool near the kitchen breakfast bar.

Cameron cracked her first crab leg. She checked off two characteristics in his favor, a good cook and a man that cleaned.

"Not a big 'Hen' drinker, huh?" Corey laughed to himself. He leaned against the kitchen sink sipping his cognac. "So what you been up to? I haven't seen or heard from you in a while."

"Whose fault is that?" Cameron asked sarcastically.

"*What*? Are you blaming me now?" Corey asked.

"If my memory serves me correctly, I was coming by last time we talked, but you never called me back."

"Well, why didn't you call me?"

"Whatever Corey, don't try to put this back on me. You sounded like you were busy that night and you were *supposed* to call me when your boys left. I called you back, and they were still here."

"See, I don't even remember all that."

"You wouldn't remember," Cameron ended the conversation. This was a new year and a new beginning for the two of them. "Let's just not focus on the past."

"That sounds good. We just won't talk about it." Corey picked up the rest of his bottle and headed out the kitchen. "When you finish, come down to the basement. I got something I wanna show you."

"Okay." Cameron yelled with shrimp stuffed in her mouth. "Wait, I'll come now."

Cameron walked down the stairs of the basement moments after Corey. "Corey, this is nice. You did this by yourself?" Corey had transformed his basement into a small studio. The light fixtures held blue light bulbs, which gave the studio a dark and drafty ambiance. Posters were pinned up everywhere, vinyl records, turntables, CDs, microphones. Everything in Corey's basement reminded Cameron of music and being an artist. Cameron never visualized it, but this felt like home to her.

"I had a little help. P-Body came through for a couple of hours on some days."

Cameron sat near the keyboard and fiddled with a couple of notes.

"Tell me what you think about this?" Corey replayed a beat he had composed.

After listening to the instrumental of what Cameron assumed to be a ballad, she commented. "I like it." She smiled, "Where are the lyrics?"

"I haven't wrote 'em yet. I got the hook but I didn't write the lyrics. The beat is tight, right?" Corey watched Cameron swaying to the beat.

"It sounds like a platinum hit. Let me hear the hook."

Corey belted out a rich, soulful hook, "Let me make you comfortable."

Corey's voice raised the small bumps on

Cameron's arms. "You gotta let me write the lyrics to this song."

"Okay, take it away." Corey smiled as he continued repeating the hook of the song and moving closer to Cameron. Her eyes remained shut as she envisioned the words for the track.

"Come here." When Cameron opened her eyes, she was face to face with Corey. His eyes locked hers. He moved from her eyes to her lips and gently kissed her.

"I'm right here." She whispered back to him.

"No, you're not 'cause I can't feel you." Corey continued grabbing her by her waist to bring her closer. Cameron kept her feet planted and an arm's distance away.

"Why you actin' all scared, like you're afraid to come close to me? Are you scared?" He teased her.

"I am not scared of you Corey." She said in an attempt to convince herself it were true. She felt immobilized by the touch of his hands around her waist. He gently pulled her out of her seat but this time she entwined herself in his arms. She came closer to him, embracing the intensity of his heart near hers, and his breath on her nose, moving down to her lips. She engaged in the passion of the moment. She parted her lips to receive his. Her mind told her to stop but her body wanted to indulge in more of the sensuous kissing.

Corey's phone rang.

"Are you going to answer it?" Cameron asked between kisses.

"Do you want me to?" Corey softly whispered.

"Yes." Cameron answered relieved to take a break from the heated moment to allow her enough time to think about her actions.

"Damn." Corey released Cameron and picked up the cordless phone. "Yo-yo- yo! What up?" Corey stared at Cameron while conversing on the phone. "Yeah, I'm here chillin' with Cameron."

He paused.

"Oh you on your way right now?"

He paused again.

"Okay I'll see you in a minute."

Corey hung up the phone and walked back towards Cameron, standing where he left her. He grabbed her by her waist again. "That was P-Body. He's on his way to lay some tracks down. You sure you don't want a drink?"

"I'm sure."

Corey kissed her again and headed towards the stairs.

"I think I'm going to head home," Cameron called out to him.

"Why?" He turned around quickly, "You can stay with me tonight."

"I got work in the morning and school in the afternoon. It's probably better if I leave now."

"Fine; suit yourself."

Corey walked up the stairs, leaving Cameron with her thoughts and the beat still playing from his song.

Cameron's cell phone started ringing.

"Where are you?" LaShaun demanded.

"Huh?"

"*Hoochie*, you heard me!" LaShaun started chuckling, "Tony just called here. He had a question about today's lecture and needed your help."

"Oh, yeah I'm-I'm on my way home." Cameron could barely keep from stuttering

"It sounds like you're at the club. What is that music playing in the background?"

"Look, I'll talk to you when I get home."

"When is that?" LaShaun insisted.

"I'll be home in a minute."

"You better bring your ass home too."

"Bye *mom!*" Cameron hung up the phone. She

would have to catch up with Corey later. LaShaun calling and P-Body being on his way were not mere coincidences. Everything happened in perfect timing. She walked up the stairs as Corey opened the front door.

P-Body came in with a couple of friends in tote behind him. Cameron went to the closet to grab her coat.

"Oh, you not speaking Cameron?" P-Body put her on the spot.

"Hey, P-Body, how are you doing?" She answered cordially.

"I'm cool, good seeing you." P-Body sat on the couch, took a bottle of beer out of a plastic bag and a bag of bud out of another. The other two followed P-Body's lead and began emptying the tobacco out of two cigars.

"You too," Cameron responded.

Corey helped Cameron put on her coat. "You know you don't have to leave," he whispered in her ear.

Cameron looked around at Corey's present company. "What am I supposed to do? Sit here and smoke one?"

"You are more than welcome," Corey teased her.

"Thanks for the offer but that's all right. I enjoyed you. I'll call you when I finish the song."

"Okay." Corey kissed her on the lips again. "Call me when you get home."

"I will." Cameron walked out the door ecstatic about the chances of her and Corey actually maintaining a relationship this time around. If he kept it up, he could just be the one.

Chapter 16 a dreadful past

Tomiko paced her office floor, about facing from one end of the wall to the next with one hand on her hip and the tip of a pen held in her mouth with the other. She had thirty minutes before her conference call with Chad McIntyre, CEO of Urban Gear. Tomiko's proposal changed the infrastructure of the Chicago based fashion firm in order to make it more visible in the market. Urban Gear produced small volume merchandise for boutiques selling their products across the country s. The proposal implicated national and international sales volumes.

Tomiko met Chad during a social event held by one of Michael's business groups; this particular organization happened to be an esteemed conglomerate of influential men in the Atlanta area. Chad, a native of Atlanta, moved to Chicago to study at Northwestern on a football scholarship, and became quite the executive after completing his studies. Since their initial acquaintance, he met Tomiko several times in Atlanta and Chicago to discuss the vision of the company and the benefits of working with a small newly incorporated firm such as Wallace & Baker. Tomiko convinced him that under her leadership, Urban Gear's transformation into a nationally recognized name brand was inevitable. There was only one thing she needed to make this deal a success, a celebrity endorsement.

On her last pace towards her desk, she sat down in her office chair, dropped her pen and picked up the receiver of her phone.

"LaShaun Johnson speaking," she answered on the first ring.

Tomiko sighed in relief at the sound of LaShaun's voice on the other line and not an answering service. After New Year's Eve at the Poetry Lounge, Tomiko decided to distance herself for a while. However, today she needed a significant favor from LaShaun.

"LaShaun, what's up girl? Happy New Year!"

"What's up stranger? I thought you were mad at me too. I haven't seen you since New Year's Eve."

"Oh, it's only been three weeks since the start of the new year so stop being dramatic and acting like it's been such a long time."

"You know we are used to you coming around by now. Cameron told me about you and her falling out. So are you alright?"

"I was never really mad at her. I'm just tired of being judged by everyone. I'm just trying to be a better me and I don't need people to remind me of my past. I'm not that girl anymore and I don't want to hear about it or be teased about it."

"I hear what you sayin'. It's amazing because I remember a time when you didn't even let what other people thought about you bother you. I know you guys will get over it and everything will be back to normal."

Tomiko interrupted LaShaun's mother hen moment. She sincerely wanted to reconcile the wrongs in her life but there was no reason to harp on the past. She wanted to focus on decisions and opportunities that helped her improve personally and accomplish her career goals. She had to move forward and what better way to do that than to land this deal with Urban Gear.

"Anyway, I didn't call you about that. I need Jason's number from you." Tomiko normally would not ask LaShaun for this type of favor, but her friend's network and connections were not off limits for this deal.

LaShaun raised her voice in suspicion of Tomiko's hidden agenda, "What do you want to talk to Jason about?"

"Since you must know, I'm working on a project here and I need his help. "

"Are you terminally ill?" LaShaun chuckled, "I mean is something wrong? You want Jason to help you with something. I just can't imagine the two of you working on anything together."

"I wouldn't actually be working with him. I'd be more working through him. I need his connection with Young-T for a client I'm working with, Urban Gear, and I need it, like yesterday." Tomiko pleaded.

"You're joking?" LaShaun paused, "Right?"

Tomiko imagined the wrinkled nose and pointed eyebrows in a fit of confusion on LaShaun's face. "LaShaun, I have never been so for real. I'm talking about making partner here, handling a multi-million dollar project and I need you like never before."

"Ok, I'll talk to him about it." LaShaun calmly replied.

"No sweetie, I need the number. I gotta talk to him myself." Tomiko was adamant about being the one to talk to Jason.

"You don't trust me to tell him what you need?"

"It's not a matter of trust. I have way more details about this venture than I can even begin to explain to you and I need to talk to him myself."

"Ok, ok! I'll give you the number but there's a catch."

"LaShaun, did you just hear me say this is a multi-million dollar project? No catches, I need to speak with Jason."

"I want you and Cameron to start talking again and since you say you aren't really mad, you have to come to the house to get the number. See ya'!"

"No, LaShaun…."

Click, was the last thing Tomiko heard before the dial tone. Tomiko began to redial LaShaun's work number when she peeked up to see Mr. Wallace looking into her office.

"Hey kiddo, you got a minute?" Mr. Wallace reminded Tomiko of her other eminent career goal, making partner at the firm. Today, he would recommend her partnership at the firm but she needed approval from the other decision makers in the firm in order to become an official partner. The meeting to decide her future at the firm was scheduled to take place strategically after her meeting with Urban Gear. The Urban Gear and the partner's meeting played a significant role in her career advancement and escalated her anxiety.

Tomiko placed the receiver back on the phone hook and waved Mr. Wallace into her office. "Please, I always have time for you. What's going on? How can I help you today?"

I just came to check on my all-star player. I know this is a big day for you and I just wanted to see how you were doing?"

"I'm just great Mr. Wallace; I mean Henry," Tomiko smiled faintly at him.

"You may be great, but you're not convincing." Henry rocked on his back heel and placed his hands in the pocket of his suit pants.

She sighed, "I'm really fine, just trying to get

some last minute meetings confirmed before the conference call in twenty minutes."

"Tomiko," He sat in one of the two chairs across from her desk and folded his arms over his belly. "You know, when I first hired you I had no idea what I was getting into. You were sharp, vibrant, young, and smart and I knew you had the credentials to make a great consultant and maybe even partner one day. You came to this company and from your first day, you put one hundred plus percent into everything that you did here. Believe me when I tell you it hasn't gone unnoticed. Every chance I get, I let the other managing partners know how valuable you are to this team. I know today is a big day for you but don't worry about any of that today. You give this your best, just like you do everything else. I know you'll get it. You'll get exactly what you've worked for and I fully support you."

He stood up and headed towards the door to exit the office. Tomiko called out to him, "Thanks Henry; for everything."

He winked at her and knowingly replied, "Go get 'em!"

Tomiko sat back in her chair and rested her arms on the armrests. She stared at the presentation she and the team had developed for the newly submitted Urban Gear proposal. Tomiko pressed the orange intercom button on her phone and dialed David, her assistant.

"Meet me in the exec board room in five minutes."

"Yes ma'am."

Tomiko heard the phone hang up and cringed. She told him numerous times to stop calling her ma'am. She knew that David would eventually break the habit of calling her ma'am; just as she learned to do when Mr. Wallace insisted she call him Henry.

Tomiko grabbed her presentation and coffee mug from her desk. She walked out her office door and down the halls to the boardroom.

Five minutes before the conference presentation, her entire team made it into the boardroom. At 10:30, she nodded for David to call Chad. A representative from marketing, accounting and legal all presented their areas of expertise to Chad McIntyre and the team at Urban Gear over the phone. They explained the budget and legal implications of a national market entry strategy.

"Chad, with you wanting to cover a larger market area, we've proposed that you launch several national campaigns and change the infrastructure of your current limited liability corporation to a full corporation. It will allow you more visibility and less risk as an owner. As a corporation, you also open up other fundraising mechanisms for advertisement campaigns and building acquisitions. We are prepared to negotiate endorsement deals with some celebrities we think will make your brand more marketable." Tomiko informed him.

"I'm very confident in the information that was presented to me in this proposal." Chad replied. "Tomiko, your team did a very thorough job and I must say I was already going to accept this proposal after it was delivered to me prior to the Christmas holiday but I'm sure I want to continue working with you and the team at Wallace & Baker for the next phase of the Urban Gear expansion."

"Chad, we are honored to work with you. Thank you so much for your time and happy New Year! David will be in touch with you so we can get the project started."

"Sounds good, we will see you soon. Give Michael my regards."

"I will; we will talk soon." Tomiko hung up the phone and clapped her hands together, "Well congratulations team. You just earned yourself more work to do! Good job everyone."

Tomiko instructed her assistant to follow-up with the partners at the firm and Chad. "David, get those MOUs up to Mr. Baker and Mr. Wallace for their signatures, and send them off to Mr. McIntyre overnight express with an invoice. I'll need you to make an appointment for a meeting with legal and accounting this afternoon. Let's meet right after lunch, around two o'clock."

When she made it back to her office, her voice mail light blinked. She checked her messages to find Keisha, Charlotte's cousin, called her. She was unable to reach Charlotte over the holiday and she wanted to know her friend and godson were safe. After listening to the urgent message, she immediately called Keisha back. "Hi Keisha, it's Tomiko. What's going on girl?"

There was silence on the phone. Then, Keisha stuttered, "N-n-nothing much." Tomiko knew Keisha always stuttered when she was uncomfortable or nervous.

"Come on Keisha, let it out." Tomiko urged her to speak.

"Y-y-ya'll always put me in the middle of your shit."

"Yeah, yeah; what's up with Charlotte? Give me the scoop." Tomiko rushed her.

"Charlotte is u-u-u-upset man."

"What's new? What is she upset about this time?"

"She found out that you-you-you've been sleeping with Devin a-a-a-an-and you know Charlotte can be co-co-co-conniving and spiteful. She had better not find out that I told you this, Tomiko!" Keisha had managed to say it all in one breath, with little stuttering. Tomiko was impressed, but knew she had to calm her down.

"Keisha, it's cool. I'm not going to say anything to her about this call. I thought something happened to her over the holiday." Tomiko noticed Henry walking towards her office. "Look, I'll have to call you back later. I gotta go."

"Tomiko, be sure to watch your back. You-you-you know Charlotte can get kind of crazy, and I have a feeling she's going to do something stupid."

"For her sake, she better be cool. I gotta go." She hung up the phone before he reached her door. He walked into the office and closed the door.

"Four to two vote, in your favor." The older man smiled kindly at Tomiko.

"Are you saying I made partner?" Four of the six partners were confident in her abilities as a partner. Tomiko barely grasped the meaning of his words. Her boss had walked in and announced to her that she achieved exactly what she wanted at the firm. "Is that what you're telling me? I'm a partner?" Tomiko confirmed excitedly.

Henry nodded his head enthusiastically, "Yes, young lady. You are the new managing partner for Wallace and Baker. This role doesn't come lightly. We will have a partner's retreat this summer. Bring your significant other. We're going to have a good time."

He winked and walked out the door. Tomiko collapsed into her desk chair and clutched her chest. She had a dichotomous moment. Tears waited to fall from her eyes and shouts of joy hinged on the edge of her tongue. She was the seventh partner of the firm. She would have to deal with Charlotte later.

After a long celebratory day at the office, Tomiko was finally ready to go home. As usual, she was the last one out of her office building. She took the elevator to the garage of the main floor.

Mr. Franklin was on the phone when he waved to her from his station. He quickly opened his window to make sure she knew he was available to chat, "Did you need an escort to your car?"

Tomiko turned and waved him off. "No, I'll be fine. I'll see you tomorrow Mr. Franklin." She used her card key to leave the office building and enter into the garage. As she walked towards her car, she heard footsteps running behind her.

When she turned to face the sound, an extreme blow to her face knocked her off her feet. She stumbled to the ground trying to release the pocketknife attached to her keys but she fumbled and dropped them with the force of another blow. The blows to her face and upper body came repeatedly. Her only source of defense to withstand the pounding was to cover her head and curl her body into a fetal position. She could not even scream for help. She thought the beating would never end until she heard a voice call out.

"Charlie, that's enough! Let's go!" It was a male voice.

"No, I want this bitch to know who I am and who she's fucking with." Charlie was a female. "Bitch, you hear me!"

The word she heard many times before as a salutatory greeting was sharpened and venomous. It was like living a nightmare. The unknown male voice came in stronger and tried to wrestle Charlie away from Tomiko. "Let's go before we get caught. They have cameras and security all over the place."

Charlie spit on Tomiko as she walked off, "Don't ever fuck with me and my family again. I thought you were much smarter than that, Corporate America Bitch; next time, no one will be around to save yo' ass."

Tomiko heard the footsteps running away from her, becoming more distant. Her face lay against the cool parking lot pavement. She shivered and thought about the possibility of not making it. She heard sirens, and then nothing else.

Chapter 17 used to love him

LaShaun enjoyed her first Friday away from work since Southern National Bank's employee lay-off two months ago. Her regular shift was Sunday through Thursday. However, when the telemarketing firm she worked for fired her upper level manager she assumed more responsibilities; including working on her regular off days. Financial businesses suffered the most from the downtrodden economy and downsizing became the new strategy of survival for these companies. LaShaun was frustrated with the daily drama at her work place. Working for her company was stressful. Her plans after graduating from college were to work with an accounting firm, not helping people to accrue more debt through credit card accounts.

However, today LaShaun chose to think about what she would wear for the upcoming Young-T album release party. In a week, she was attending the highly publicized event. Jason's imperfections were evident to LaShaun. He was not the most sensitive man she ever dated, but random outings like this and New Year's Eve made up for his personality flaws. She knew he could give her the lifestyle and relationship she often fantasized about if she just remained patient and gave him what he wanted. Even if she had not seen him in the weeks leading up to the party, at least he called her and reassured her they would be going.

LaShaun picked up the phone receiver and dialed her coconspirator.

"Hello," Reese groggily answered the phone.

"What are you doing?"

"Nothing but getting some beauty rest. What time is it?" Reese yawned. "I need to get my butt up and clean this place."

"It's nine o'clock. What are you doing later?"

"Later, like what time?"

"This afternoon, I need your help and I thought that you may want to come to the mall with me."

"What you gotta get from the mall?"

LaShaun could here Reese's voice perk up at the mention of shopping, "Just something for this party I'm going to next week."

"Ooooh, a party! I wanna go."

LaShaun had Reese's full attention. "Well I would tell you to come on but Jason invited me. It's supposed to be some party for Young-T. You know the rapper that came out with that new single, 'This is Why We Ride.'"

"That's right." Reese reminded LaShaun, "You know every well-known person in the music industry is attending that party. It's all over the radio. You should be honored Jason invited you."

"Yeah, I'm pretty excited about it. Are you going?"

"This party promoter I'm kickin' it with is supposed to be doing all the advertising and he said we are going. I don't know though. You know how that can go down. Brothas act like they got it going on like that and really end up being the person passing out the flyers for the party, talking 'bout 'Yeah I'm a promoter.'"

LaShaun had to laugh at that because she knew what Reese meant. Everyone had a business card and was supposedly somebody big time.

"Are you and Jason an item now?

"Girl, I guess. Who knows what this boy is up to next, but I am sure going to enjoy it while it lasts."

"That's my girl!" Reese agreed in support of LaShaun's decision to continue dating Jason. "Well, don't be surprised if you see me at the party, especially if ol' boy really has some plug. The party should give me some good exposure."

"You never stop do you?" LaShaun thought about the time she went with Reese to an open model call in Miami. They paid the event organizers hundreds of dollars to meet modeling agents face to face and neither of them were selected by a talent agency. They later learned the golden rule of the entertainment industry, 'legitimate agencies will not ask for upfront fees to represent talent.' LaShaun decided to give up on the model call but Reese continued to pursue her dreams.

"So are you coming with me? What time will you be ready?" LaShaun asked Reese.

"Yeah, let's do it. I'll be ready in about two hours. That should give me enough time to get myself together."

LaShaun looked at the clock, calculating the minutes it would take both her and Reese to be ready. "How about I meet you at the mall at noon?"

"Alright, bet."

LaShaun hung up the phone, turned off the TV and turned on her music. She had some cleaning up to do herself. Right before she got into her groove, the phone rang. The number was unfamiliar to her but she decided to answer it anyway.

"Hello?" She answered apprehensively.

"Shaun."

"*Andre*?" She instantly recognized her ex-boyfriend's voice. She last spoke to him two years ago when he gave her back the keys to the apartment they lived in together.

"I see you remembered me," he laughed. "Are you busy?"

"No, not really." LaShaun surprised herself at her calm demeanor. "Where have you been?" She asked cordially.

"Right now I'm in LA."

"You moved back out there?"

"Yeah, it was getting' crazy in the A.T.L. I had to come out here and clear my head. I heard through the grapevine you ran into Corey."

"I ran into him at a New Year's spot while I was hanging out with Cameron. I haven't hung out with him for a minute. He and Cameron started dating again, I guess. You know your boy be trippin'."

"Oh, why it gotta be like that?" Andre asked as they both laughed as he mustered up the strength to admit the purpose of his call. "Shaun, I've been thinking about you a lot over the past couple of months."

"*Really*?" LaShaun asked, surprised to hear the confession. When they broke up, she could care less if he ever called again. Although she wondered what he did after they broke up; she never reached out to him because it would rehash memories she tried to suppress. However, today she found herself curious and desiring to know why he would still think about her.

"Yeah, when Corey told me he ran into you I asked him for your number."

"I see, well, I have to tell Corey off the next time I run into him. He can't just be givin' my number out."

"Oh, you didn't want me to have your number?"

"I mean, it's really hard for me to answer that right now. We didn't actually end our relationship on good terms."

"I know, I'm reminded of it every day." An awkward silence fell over the phone. Andre cleared his throat and continued, "What else have you been up to?"

"Workin', chillin', the usual," LaShaun answered casually

"I see."

"What about you? What are you doing in Cali?"

"Well I am working, thinking about you a lot, you know? I just want to let you know that I miss you and I hated the way things ended for us. I'm…" He left a long pause, "I'm sorry for not being the man you needed me to be back then."

"Andre, you don't have to apologize." LaShaun silently prayed that she would not cry over the phone. She did not want this phone call to cause her any undue stress by reliving the hurtful events of the past.

"No, let me finish," Andre continued. "When you told me that you wouldn't have my child, it hurt me. It was like a blow to my heart. A feeling I couldn't even describe. I was angry because, to me, that showed you didn't care much about our relationship and for you to be able to disregard my baby so easily, it hurt. I just felt like shit."

"I don't know what you want me to say. What did you think would happen when I saw you out with another woman? You left me no choice and when I needed you, you weren't *there*. I couldn't trust that or you. When it was over, I felt like that was probably the best decision for me at time. I didn't want to end up taking care of a child by myself."

Andre hurt her in a way that no other man could or would, because she would not allow another man to come that close to her again. Tears streamed down her face, burning the corners of her eyes as she reminisced on the painful break up.

Andre interjected, "I didn't have a choice but to leave. You did kick me out the house. It was never my intention to leave you."

The words resonated around her heart and sunk into her soul. She believed him and it made her conjure up feelings of regret she felt only once, right after the abortion of her unborn child. She forgave him, they were both young and she never questioned Andre's sincerity. However, his fidelity was indeed in question.

"Shaun, I'll be in town in a couple of weeks and I want to see you."

"Dre, I have to think about that, I don't know if I'm ready for it."

"Think about it and I'll call you. Okay?"

"Yeah, okay."

She never found peace in her heart over her decision. In order to live with it, she acted as if it never happened. She knew that she could love the child, but being a single mother was never her desire or intention. She had endured too much pain. She deeply wanted to be able to trust someone again but nothing could bring back what she had lost two years ago.

LaShaun waited for Reese in the food court of Lenox Mall. She took a seat in front of the pretzel vendor, preoccupied with the conversation she had with Andre. He brought back some painful memories.

She spotted Reese coming down the escalator toward the food court. Reese waved once they made eye contact.

The two of them settled on shopping at one of the anchor, larger department stores in the mall. LaShaun went through racks of clothing, aimlessly searching for the perfect outfit. Reese decided to spend the time reflecting on her love life.

"I just don't know Shaun, this dating scene is

played. I'm tired of going in and out of relationships. I just want someone I can spend the rest of my life with and who will support me in my career so I don't have to work like this." Reese looked over at LaShaun noticeably not paying her any attention. "I think I'm going skinny dipping on the moon." Reese said to get a reaction. "What do you think about that?"

LaShaun nodded her head in agreement, "Wait what did you say?"

"So, what's wrong with you?"

Taking in a deep breath, LaShaun decided to tell Reese about her phone call. "Andre called me."

"Your *ex*!" Reese had only been around to see the end of LaShaun's break up with Andre.

"Yes, he said he is coming into town in a few weeks."

"Shut up! Why? Is he coming back for you?"

"Just to visit some old friends, at least that is what I'm thinking. He didn't really say."

"Girl, he is coming back for you. That boy ain't coming just to visit."

"Reese, don't say that."

"I'm telling you what I know, not what I heard. All of a sudden, he's coming in town to visit. I know he wants to see you."

"I mean, yeah, but that doesn't mean anything."

"What are you going to tell Jason?"

"I'm not going to tell him a damn thing. What he doesn't know won't hurt him."

"You are doing the right thing. It will only make matters worse. I talked to him the other day ya' know?"

"Who?"

"Jason, he told me that he wanted you to open up and blah, blah, blah. I told him to talk to you. You all need to spend more time together."

"So this is why he is taking me out. He thinks he's slick."

"Don't trip. Ya'll both need to sit down and talk to each other. Relationships don't just work themselves out, people work them out."

LaShaun wanted to get closer to Jason, but his overbearing attitude made it difficult for her to express herself at times. It flattered her to know he wanted the same thing she wanted from their relationship but she wished he talked to her about it.

If she could combine Andre's admiration for her with Jason's lifestyle and credentials, she would have a perfect mate. She knew she could not have both worlds with either one of them.

"Thanks for coming with me Reese. I really needed this."

"That's what friends are for. There's nothing like a little shop therapy." Reese placed her arm around LaShaun and squeezed her shoulders. "And don't worry too much about Andre or Jason. Just have a good time. That's what life is about. You aren't married to either of them. So don't stress yourself out."

"I know that's right." LaShaun grabbed a denim jean outfit and held it up for Reese to give her opinion on it.

"That's it girl." Reese pulled on the three quarter length denim jacket and pointed to the lighter brown stitching on the seams. "All you need is some camel color boots to set off this stitching. You got a purse to match?"

"My Coach bag," LaShaun smiled.

"Are you paying with cash, check or credit?" Reese and LaShaun laughed on the way to the registers.

Chapter 18 making the grade

Cameron's stomach became queasy at the thought of meeting with her professor this early in the school year. Graduation was only a few months away. The only measure of performance Mr. Mahoney could assess her on was the quiz they had taken the previous week on Theories of Management. Nevertheless, a meeting called by the professor did not usually mean anything good. She knew a combination of Corey and school was much more than she could handle this semester.

Cameron pulled into the school parking deck and quickly walked across the acres of campus, with its meticulously manicured landscape, to get to the business school. She had scheduled the appointment for nine in the morning, which gave her ten minutes to get there.

Cameron walked across the marble flooring of the business school's foyer, up the mahogany trimmed staircase, and into the office of Mr. Mahoney, her professor. Tracie, Mr. Mahoney's administrative assistant, brushed the blonde hair from her eyes and placed a hair clip on the back of her head to hold it up.

"Now, that's better." Tracie made the statement as if the two women were continuing a previous conversation, "Hi Cameron, how are ya'?" she asked in her usually pleasant southern drawl.

Cameron tried to appear unmoved by her current situation. Mr. Mahoney had not discussed the intent of their meeting. "I have a nine o'clock with Mr. Mahoney."

"Yes you do." Tracie smiled and that gave Cameron a sense of relief. "I'll buzz him for you. He's meeting with another student right now."

Great, I'm not the only one, Cameron thought comforting herself.

The door of the office opened five minutes later. Her stomach jumped back to her chest. The anticipation made her more aware of her internal organs; she felt every palpitation of her heart and the steady movement of her diaphragm.

Tony walked out of the office and Mr. Mahoney followed two steps behind him. Tony shook his hand and glanced at Cameron.

"Cameron, I'll see you now." Mr. Mahoney greeted her and walked back into his office.

"Hey Tony," Cameron grabbed her belongings and mentally prepared for her mysterious meeting.

"Cameron, it's okay." Tony touched her forearm to reassure her she was safe. Cameron could never play poker. She wore her feelings vividly in her facial expressions. She took a deep breath.

"A couple of us are hanging out at The Pub tonight. We'll have a couple of beers and celebrate our last semester at this place. Be strong Pookie."

Cameron shook her head in agreement, "If God is for me, who can be against me, right?"

"That's what I'm talking about." Tony smiled, "I'll see you tonight."

"Okay."

Cameron walked into the office towards Mr. Mahoney's desk. He reviewed a stack of papers on his desk, one of the sheets had Cameron's name on the top.

"Ms. Turner, how are your classes going?"

"It's a little hard to determine right now, since we've only been in school a few weeks. It seems like it's flying by, but I feel like I'm doing pretty good." Cameron subconsciously admitted that her personal life distracted her from her schoolwork. She hung out more, writing her poetry to keep herself from fantasizing about Corey. She was barely devoting enough time to her studies.

"Well, this is a preemptive meeting. I don't want you to be alarmed, because you have plenty of time to bring your grade back up by the end of the semester. Your first quiz you scored fifty-nine out of a hundred. I've spoken to some of the other professors, and they seemed to think you are a sharp student. This concerns me because this is your last semester and you have to pass this class with a B or better to graduate.

"Now, I'm willing to provide you with some resources if you need them. My office hours are set up so that students can come in with any questions. If you find yourself lost or falling behind, come see me." Mr. Mahoney peered at Cameron with his hazel eyes. He sat back in his chair and rocked a little, holding a pen at his chest between his index and middle finger.

"I'm inclined to believe my colleagues. I know you can pass this class but there is a lot of reading involved. You have to do the reading on your own time to keep up with the pace of the class. Do you have the textbook?"

Cameron shook her head to confirm she purchased the book. She had not made a grade below a C since her high school senior year in calculus and was discouraged at the thought of failing. She hated being below average in anything. She needed to make some minor adjustments in her schedule and life. First thing, no more Corey daydreams. Secondly, she would have to visit the poetry venues less often. She would devote more time to her studies.

"Great, well did you have any questions for me? Are there some concepts that you don't understand?"

"No, I just need to find another method of studying. I'm probably not focusing on the main concepts. That's all. I will look over my test and try to figure out what may have happened."

Mr. Mahoney gave Cameron her test. "I look forward to this grade coming up Ms. Turner. I want to see the student that everyone else is bragging about."

Cameron smiled. "You will Mr. Mahoney." Cameron gathered her bags and walked to the office door. "Thanks."

"No problem. I'll see you at ten for class."

"Okay."

Cameron's school day ended at six o'clock in the evening. She was feeling overwhelmed and consumed at the thought of not being successful in Mr. Mahoney's course. After classes, she met Tony and sat with him at The Pub bar.

Tony ordered a pitcher of beer for them to share. "So, what's the deal? Why did you meet with Mahoney?"

"He called the meeting." Cameron didn't want to discuss her personal failures, especially not with Tony, whom she usually assisted with his class work.

"He called a meeting with several students. You know the common denominator of all the students he called."

Cameron shook her head, "No, what?"

The bartender placed the golden tap beer in front of them and filled two glasses.

"We're all black."

"What?" Cameron, with a look of astonishment, put her glass of beer to her lips and sipped. She wiped her mouth and pushed the tap away. *I don't drink beer,* she thought to herself.

"Yup, all the students he called in to meet with him." Tony raised his hand and released a finger for every person he mentioned, "Me, you, Chris, LaTonya, Rochelle, Amina, and Ngozi."

"I don't believe it. Are you saying there's something discriminatory going on?" Cameron smacked her lips in disbelief, "No, he wouldn't have made it so obvious."

"I didn't say he called all the black students. There is still Michael and Alexandria that he didn't call. Anyway," Tony looked up at the door and spotted the other students he had invited. "Here they come now."

"Tony!" Chris and Tony shook hands and gave each other a hug, "What's poppin'?"

"Chris, you know Cameron." Tony pointed to Cameron who was seated next to him.

"Yeah, what's up?" Chris hugged Cameron around her shoulders while she remained seated.

"Where's Ngozi?" Cameron asked LaTonya as all the peers greeted each other.

"I don't know. She said she wasn't feeling it and she had to go lie down."

"Are we going to protest or something?" Cameron asked the group.

"Well, all I'm saying is that I'm not doing anything that's going to jeopardize my graduation. I got family coming from all over for this." LaTonya sat on the bar stool next to Cameron.

"I just say we go to the Dean and talk to him about it." Chris interjected.

"Do we even have anything to prove that this teacher is racially biased?" Cameron asked.

"Do you see anyone in the group that doesn't

look like you?" Chris raised his arms and offered Cameron the opportunity to observe the people around her.

He made a good point. Cameron wanted nothing more but to receive a fair and impartial grade. She already experienced similar situations at the school, but she didn't realize that it was happening to other students like her and that they were ready to assemble and get questions answered on their behalf.

"Okay, here's the game plan. We need to get a hold of one of the other students' tests and compare our answers and grades with theirs. It's the only way we can prove these tests are subjective and are not being graded fairly."

"Who is close enough to any of the other students to get the test?" LaTonya asked.

Tony looked at Cameron.

"I'm not close to anyone. Josh was the only other person that I dealt with, and he's not here anymore."

Everyone looked at Cameron as if she were the last hope. "Fine I'll see what I can do." Cameron raised her hand in surrender. Josh would think she went completely insane after he left Atlanta, but Cameron was down for the cause.

Chapter 19 heal the pain

Tomiko woke up with a nagging pain in her side. She moaned and noticed she was not in a room by herself; she raised her hand to her head and hit her cheek with the cords from an IV. The nurse rushed to her bedside in response to her moans.

"Are you okay Ms. Bordeaux?" Tomiko shook her head. The nurse pressed a button on her IV, "That should make you feel better in just a minute."

"Why am I here?" Tomiko asked groggily.

"You suffered a mild concussion. You blacked out for a minute but you are fine now. You're at Georgia Southern Hospital."

"*Southern Hospital!*" Tomiko exclaimed.

"You are at one of the best trauma centers in the nation my dear. Would you rather be somewhere else?"

Tomiko realized her outburst might have been somewhat offensive "No, I am fine here." She could feel the pain medicine beginning to work. "What did you give me?"

"A little morphine-"the nurse handed her a small white device with a blue button on top of it. "Whenever you feel pain just hold this button down and you can dispense at your own free will. Doctor Williams will be with you in a moment to discuss your condition. Is there anyone I can call for you?"

"Could you call my fiancé?" Tomiko knew she would have to tell Michael what happened. There was no way she would ever be able to hide the scratches on her face and the bruises on her body.

"Sure, I'll give him a call. And lucky for you those robbers didn't take that pretty ring you got sittin' on your finger."

A robber? Is that what happened. I was a victim of robbery. Tomiko thought to herself while looking down at her hand to see her ring still there.

"Yeah. Lucky for me," Tomiko replied.

The nurse handed her a notepad to write Michael's number.

Tomiko handed it back to her grimacing.

"Don't move too much, I'll be right back."

She noticed a bouquet of soft pink, yellow and white tulips sat on her windowsill. She wondered who could have possibly known she was in the hospital already. The door opened. The doctor and a man dressed in a dark suit entered her room.

"Hello Ms. Bordeaux. I'm Dr. Williams and this is Detective Robert Martin. He wants to ask you a few questions about your encounter last night. I'm here to make sure that you are strong enough to answer these questions. How are you feeling?"

"I'm okay. I guess I'm just a little confused."

"It's okay. You suffered a minor concussion and your ribs are bruised, but nothing is broken. You should be back to your old self in no time. Do you feel up to answering some questions?"

"Sure." Tomiko tried to readjust herself to be

more attentive. The doctor gestured for her to remain in a comfortable position and relax.

"Ms. Bordeaux, I just need to find out what happened last night. We suspected robbery, but we found nothing on the suspects we apprehended and your wallet and other valuables remained by your side at the scene of the assault. Do you know why anyone would want to physically harm you?"

"No, I have no idea."

"Ma'am, do you know these two people?" The detective pulled out two mug shots. They were pictures of a man she never met before and Charlotte.

"Yes I know the girl."

"How do you know her?"

"She is a friend of mine from up north."

"Chicago?"

"Yes."

"Ma'am, these are the two assailants we apprehended in the parking lot. Do you have any idea why either of them would have reason to do you any physical harm? Was there something that they may have said at the time of, or before the attack?"

"No." Tomiko wanted to end the interrogation. Now she remembered Charlotte's voice before she blacked out.

"Ma'am, do you want to press charges against them?"

Tomiko thought for a moment and asked curiously, "Who called you?"

"The night security called 9-1-1."

Detective Martin waited for Tomiko to answer his question. "Ms. Bordeaux, are you going to press charges?"

"I don't know. It's a lot to take in right now. Do I have to answer this right now?"

Tomiko looked at her Doctor. "No, you don't. We'll let you rest for now. Detective Martin, I'll lead you out."

"Sure," the detective reached in his inner coat pocket to hand her his business card. "Ms. Bordeaux, here's my card. If you can think of anything that could provide some answers to the motives behind this incident we'd appreciate it. Call me anytime if you have questions about the status of the case."

"I will."

Michael rushed in the room as the Doctor and Detective walked out.

"Tomiko, baby, are you okay?" He moved quickly to her bedside. "Who was the guy with the doctor?"

"Michael, I'm fine." Tomiko tried to remain strong but was not convincing. She knew if Michael sensed there was a problem, he would demand every nurse and doctor to cater to her 24/7. "What took you so long to get here?" Tomiko wanted to keep a sense of independence, even if she did really need him now. It made her feel too vulnerable.

"I came as soon as I could. I was on a conference call when the nurse initially called, but I ended it so I could make it here." He kissed her on the big lump that sat right on her forehead. "Do they know who did this to you?" Michael leaned on the bed rails.

Tomiko wished that she talked to Michael more about her past. It was a strain for her to tell him the truth now that she lay in a hospital bed. If he wanted her, he had to want everything about her, including her past.

"Yes, they know. That was the detective leaving out of here with the doctor. He told me they had two people in custody."

"Good, that's good to know they're off the streets. It's just hard to be safe anywhere now days." Michael thought about the high security of the office building. "Where was the security guard? Didn't they know you were going to your car?" Michael pulled out his cell phone and attempted to make a phone call but Tomiko reached for his arm to calm him down. The pain stopped her from fully reaching him. She grunted and Michael stopped ranting to attend to her.

"Are you okay baby? Don't try to move."

"Franklin worked the night shift and was very adamant about walking me to my car. But me being stubborn, I told him not to worry."

"Tomiko, I told you to stop acting like you don't need anyone. That stubborn independent attitude is not going to get you anywhere baby." Michael realized it was not the appropriate time to give her a lecture. He kissed her on her red and blue cheek, which was much softer than usual from the bruising. "It's okay baby. We are going to work it out. Damn!" Michael swore angrily.

"There is much more to the story. I don't know where to begin."

"Did they take anything?" His fiancé was lying in the hospital bed resembling the American flag with her face looking red, white, and blue. It tore Michael that he could do nothing to prevent or help her condition.

"I know one of the attackers."

"Who? Who are they?" Michael was shocked.

"They are a couple of people from home that I had a conflict with some years ago." Tomiko knew that Michael's understanding of her past was minimal. His family raised him in the suburbs. He went to a college preparatory high school where he was a minority. He was out of touch from the realities of Tomiko's world. "They retaliated on me at a place I thought they would be too afraid to come."

"Were you in a gang or something? I'm not following you Tomiko."

Tomiko rolled her eyes at him, "No Michael, I wasn't a gang member."

"Well than I don't understand. Are you saying this is a high school grudge?" Michael had to admit that such behavior was beyond him. He retaliated against people where they hurt the most—their pockets. He relied on the court system to serve justice. He knew she was not born into a financially stable family, but he deemed her as an exception. "Tomiko, they are so beneath you. Don't worry about those people, don't worry about it. I will do everything in my power to ensure that it is a long time before they see the light of day. They are exactly where they belong, behind bars."

She agreed with Michael. He never experienced the types of peer pressures like the ones she did in Chicago. The code of the streets called for violent matters to be resolved violently and without police interference. Tomiko had advanced along too far in her career and life. She would not be able to give Charlotte the street justice she deserved.

Cameron and LaShaun brought Tomiko fresh baked Krispy Kreme donuts. The warm glazed donuts were one of Tomiko's favorite foods. The nurse showed them the way to her door and they walked in quietly just in case she was asleep.

"Well, tell them to fax the remainder of the request to my office assistant and I will take a look at it next week." Cameron and LaShaun barely recognized Tomiko when they walked in her hospital bedroom. Tomiko was bandaged and still on the phone trying to conduct business affairs.

"Girl, if you don't get off that phone." LaShaun walked over to the side of the bed and held her hand over the button to hang up the phone. Tomiko held her finger up to bid for one minute.

"You're going to have to tell them to wait because there is nothing I can do from here." Tomiko finally hung up the phone and smiled at her friends. On the inside and out she was happy to see their faces. "I'm so happy that you guys made it. I was beginning to worry if I had any friends or not." It was Tomiko's second day in the hospital. She noticed the familiar green, white and red donut box. "Oh, what did you bring me? I've been craving these donuts. Le' me have one."

Cameron broke out the box of donuts and they each grabbed one. "So when did the doctor say you were getting out of here."

"Tomorrow, they said they want to make sure that there is nothing critically wrong with me. So far they said I just have a couple of bruised ribs and I had a mild concussion when I first came in, but believe me I look worst than I feel."

"Well that's good to know because you look terrible." LaShaun teased her friend.

Cameron elbowed LaShaun in her side.

"Forget you LaShaun." Tomiko replied.

"Did they find out what happened? Does anyone know anything?" Cameron asked.

"Yeah, Charlotte…"

"*Your friend from home*?" LaShaun asked in disbelief.

"Well, I don't know about friend, but she is definitely from home. Somehow, she found out about Devin and me, and decided she was going to whip my ass. Charlotte may have been upset about it but she should have at least given me the opportunity to talk to her about it. I wanted to tell her everything. But honestly, I would have never saw it coming. Not even from a mile away."

"So you are telling me that little run-in was about some man that you aren't even dealing with anymore?" LaShaun continued, "How could she be so juvenile. That's some high school bullshit."

"Who do you think told her?" Cameron asked.

"The only person I can think of is Devin but he was so against me bringing it up to her when I went home last year." Tomiko wiped her hands of sticky glaze from the donut. She held her hands against her face and let out a silent cry.

Cameron and LaShaun both consoled her as they stood on opposite sides of her bed with their arms around her, but Tomiko needed a long cry. It was something she had not done in years. She completely turned her emotions off and now her body was intoxicated with all the disappointment and stress she kept to herself over the years.

After moments of silence, LaShaun decided to break the ice again. "Well, I got family in Chicago. Let me know if you need me to call in a favor."

"Don't do that," Cameron demanded sharply to discourage the thought of bringing others into the conflict. "The girl is already in jail. Let the police handle it."

"Damn Cameron! I was just playing." She looked back at Tomiko, "unless you really need me to call them?"

"No, Cameron's right. It's not even worth getting other people involved." Tomiko wiped the tears from her eyes. "I really feel bad because I haven't told Michael the truth about the whole situation." Tomiko continued to sob, "I surely didn't tell him about Devin and me. Now it's all come back to blow up in my face." Tomiko struggled to regain her composure and continued wiping her face with the saturated tissue.

"It's like they say, you can take the girl out the 'hood, but you can't take the 'hood out of the girl." LaShaun replied.

"Well, you are now looking at a reformed 'hood rat." Tomiko managed to crack a joke.

It really did Tomiko's soul good to have her friends around at times like this, and they always knew exactly how to bring her spirits up. Tomiko made an allegiance that when she came out of this, she was going to stop neglecting her friends and take time to see them more and she was no longer taking Michael for granted. He was a good man and she deserved him. No matter what happened in the past, she was worthy of love.

Chapter 20 across enemy lines

Ding-Dong, the loud ring reminded Cameron she was in the store alone. Cameron placed the inventory book on the makeshift desk in the storage room. The desk was an older brown folding table with a desktop computer. Cameron estimated the computer was purchased in the early 1990s. It was at least a ten-year old model. Cameron challenged the integrity of the table whenever she placed thick five-inch, three ringed binders on top of it.

Cameron logged the date for the last supply order placed by the party store to update the inventory list. She walked into the stores retail area, straight down the center aisle featuring supplies for themed birthday parties for children. She reached the front of the store and noticed two women at the Valentine's Day display her and the owner set up moments before the store opened today.

Cameron walked over to greet them. "Hello, can I help you ladies find anything today?" Cameron frowned as she recognized the face of one of the women. "Meagan?"

Meagan held a package of napkins with red hearts across them in her hand and looked up from the price tag to greet the store salesperson. "Oh my gosh, Cameron, I didn't know you worked here."

"No, you wouldn't." Cameron smiled faintly. "What are you looking for?"

"Well, we've been asked to throw a sweetheart party for one of the fraternities on campus. Now, don't ask me which one because we've been sworn to secrecy." Meagan raised her right hand as if she were taking an oath.

"Understandable," Cameron nodded. "Are you just looking for cups and napkins or other decorations?"

"I don't know. These prices are somewhat high. Twenty-five napkins for four bucks is pretty steep don't you think?"

"Yeah, it is but it's a specialty store and these napkins have raised hearts. We have some things that are less expensive. Follow me," Cameron led Meagan to the stores valentine day aisle when she remembered her commission from the meeting at the Pub with her other classmates. "Oh, by the way, remember last semester you made mention of having the tests from previous students. Do you still have that?'

"Oh yeah," Meagan continued to follow Cameron while her friend Sarah drifted in the background, looking for other items to add to their handcarts. "What about these napkins? They still have decorations but they are a lot cheaper." Meagan showed Sarah.

"Yeah and I don't think the guys are going to care about raised hearts on the napkin. They'll probably be too drunk to think about it." Sarah raised her hand over her mouth realizing she was in the company of another student from Southern State. "Not that we're going to have liquor at the party.

"I know how the frat parties get. Believe me, you haven't told the Provost."

"Relax, Cameron's cool." Meagan assured her.

"Whew!" Sarah rolled her eyes. "I have to remember I talk too much sometimes."

"So, Meagan, you think you can get those test to me?"

"Cameron, of course; I told you last semester you could have them if you want them. Speaking of last semester, how's Josh doing? Have you talked to him lately?"

"Not lately." Cameron and Josh exchanged emails a couple of times over the past month but no phone conversations. In her last message to him, she invited him to attend her graduation and he had not replied. "How did you do on the last theories test?"

"Oh, I aced it!" Meagan laughed while looking at Sarah. "The old tests really help with studying. The questions aren't exactly the same but they are pretty close."

"Do you have a copy of your test I can look at too?'

"Why would you want my test? We already took it?"

"I just want to compare my answers to yours. I didn't do too well on it."

"Oh, I guess that's okay."

Cameron contemplated telling Meagan the entire truth about what her and the other classmates where conspiring to do in regards to the fair grading practices in the Theories of Management course. However, she feared that Meagan might be apprehensive about sharing her work if the results were used to demonstrate inequities in testing to the Dean.

"Ok, Meagan," Cameron began to confess. "We need the information to get our tests graded fairly."

"*We?*" Meagan raised her eyebrow.

"Yes, we are trying to get Mr. Mahoney to review our grades again because a handful of us didn't do so well on the test and we think he might not have graded our test as objectively as he could've."

"So, you would use my test to-"

"Just see if there were things we really missed on the test or if certain things were overlooked by Mr. Mahoney."

Meagan pondered on the scenario. Although Cameron solicited her help, she did not want to receive any backlash from the professor. "I have one condition." She replied in solution to her concern although she had not verbalized it.

"What is it?" It's not like Cameron had a choice in the matter this time. She had to comply since she was the group's choice to lobby for the tests.

"You can't mention my name or that the test I'm giving you is mine. I'll white out the name but I don't want Dean Sutherlin or Mr. Mahoney to have my name for anything." Meagan looked at Cameron to make sure she would comply with the conditions.

"Okay, no problem."Cameron promised.

"Pinky swear." Meagan raised her pinky to Cameron.

Cameron hesitantly interlocked her pinky with Meagan's and agreed to the terms. She hadn't pinky swore in years, probably since she was twelve years old. *But whatever*, she thought. She did what she had to do for the team.

"Great, I'll bring the tests tomorrow." Meagan gleefully finished filling her basket with items. "Sarah, come on I don't want to be in here forever.

"Well, you're the one doing all the talking. I think I have everything we need." Sarah replied impatiently.

"Cameron, you'll ring us up?" Meagan asked.

"Sure, come on." Cameron led the women to the

register to check them out.

"Is there a discount for students?" Sarah asked.

"Actually there is, I'll take care of you."

Disbelief consumed Cameron's mind. She and Meagan actually held a decent conversation and she realized Meagan could actually be a compassionate person. Maybe she had her pegged wrong all this time. At least this part of the mission was over. Once she received the tests, she could be done with this entire episode of her life.

"I got the test." Cameron sat down across from Tony at an empty seat at the student café located in Manor Hall. She handed him the stacks of paper.

"I knew we could depend on you Pookie." Tony looked through the papers while Cameron nervously tapped her fingers on the table.

"Well, let me know how things go and if you need me for anything else." Cameron replied after Tony began flipping through the pages of the exam.

"Oh, we aren't done. We still have to meet with Dean Sutherlin. "

"I never agreed to meet with Dean Sutherlin. My job was to get the tests. I got them so someone else should have to go with you to the meeting."

"Pookie, you have one of the highest GPAs at the school. No one is going to listen to us."

"Tony this is really not fair. I feel like I'm being put in the middle of something."

"You are in the middle of something. It's called 'failing this course' if we don't do anything about it."

Cameron sighed, propping her elbow on the table and resting her cheek on her fist. "What's the game plan?"

"We take the tests up to the Dean, point out the discrepancies in the grading and get him to have Mr. Mahoney take a second look at our grades."

"I'm glad you think it's that simple." Cameron slid her hand from under her face. "You think Dean Sutherlin is going to demand one of his instructors to re-grade our tests because we aren't happy with the scores."

"Do you have a better plan?" Tony asked emphatically.

Cameron looked around the café and didn't reply.

"Good, we have to meet him in five minutes so let's go." Tony grabbed his bag and picked up Cameron by her arm. "Pookie, let's go!"

"Fine, but I'm not saying anything when we get in the office."

"Good, you can just be my moral support." Tony smiled and kissed Cameron on her cheek.

Cameron fiercely wiped at her cheek removing the residual wetness from the kiss.

"Just think of it like this, when we're done, the only thing you have to worry about is finishing up class and preparing for our trip to the Virgin Islands."

"Wait a minute, I didn't hear about any trip to the islands."

"I told LaTonya to let you know. We are leaving two weeks after graduation. All you need is a two-hundred fifty dollar deposit." Tony continued to hold Cameron by her arm as they walked towards the Dean's office.

"That's definitely a plan. How much is the entire trip?"

"All inclusive with four to a room it's six hundred fifty which still isn't bad for the Virgin Islands."

"I agree."

"So you're in?"

"Yes, I'm in."

Tony approached the Dean's receptionist, "Hi Mrs. Wilson, we have a 9:30am with Dean Sutherlin."

Mrs. Wilson looked as if she would retire any day. She moved slowly and was not friendly like Mr. Mahoney's assistant. Cameron noticed a picture on her desk of a person who resembled her. She was thin, a stark contrast from Mrs. Wilson, with dark brown hair.

"Who is that, your daughter?" Cameron asked.

"No, it's me," She slammed the pen on the desk without looking up at the two students. "Sign in here and take a seat behind me." She pointed to a small leather bench stationed behind the reception area and near the door of Dean Sutherlin's office.

As Cameron sat down the leaves from the Phoenix roebelenii, a plant that sprawled out like a fan, swayed against her head. Cameron looked at Tony and whispered, "What is her problem?"

Tony shrugged his shoulders and whispered back, "I don't know. I don't come up here often."

Mrs. Wilson dialed the Dean by speaker, "Dr. Sutherlin, two students are here to see you for your 9:30 appointment."

"Thank you, send them in." Dean Sutherlin announced over the speaker.

"You can go in," She yelled back to them.

Tony opened the door and entered first with Cameron a few steps behind him.

"Come on in," the five-foot six-inch man welcomed them in his office. His hair was dark and eyes dark brown but nothing seemed intimidating about the notorious Dean. He seemed excited to see the two of them. Although it was their first time meeting one–on-one, he treated the two students as if they were friends he hadn't talked to in a while. He came from behind his desk, walked over to Cameron and Tony, and shook their hands.

"What are your names?" He asked while leading them to the seats near his desk.

"I'm Anthony Brown."

"…and I'm Cameron Turner. It's a pleasure to meet you Dean Sutherlin."

"Alright, Mr. Brown and Ms. Turner, what is it we need to talk about today?"

"Dean Sutherlin, we spoke with some of our fellow classmates and we believe we may not have been graded fairly on a test we recently took for a class."

"Hmm," Dean Sutherlin leaned back in his chair. "Well, I tell you," he began in defense mode. "Lots of times when students don't fare well on a test they immediately revolt against the teacher and I've been doing this for some time now, and usually, there's nothing to substantiate the accusations students make against the teachers."

"Now," Dean Sutherlin continued. "Have you met with the instructor to see if there's something you can do to better prepare for the next examination?"

"Yes, the teacher met with all the students that received a failing grade and he did let us know he would be available if we needed any extra help." Tony redirected the conversation, "but the problem is that this test wasn't graded fairly. Even when compared to other students receiving higher marks, there was no justification for the reductions we received on the exam."

Tony handed him the papers.

Dean Sutherlin looked through the tests and the answers briefly, "Well, I think the major issue to resolve here is the fact there's no grading rubric from the instructor. Is this Mr. Mahoney's Theories of Management course?"

"Yes sir," Tony and Cameron both replied.

"Well, I tell you what, I'll talk to Mr. Mahoney about distributing a rubric but you need to speak to him about the discrepancies in your grade. If you still don't get any resolution, I'd be more than happy to step in and meet with Mr. Mahoney and any of the other students involved."

Cameron looked at Tony, wanting to say, 'I told you so.' Instead, she quietly exited the office with Tony behind her.

"What did you think about that?" She asked him when they were further down the hall and out of Mrs. Wilson's sight.

"I think we got a lot of work to do before this next test." Tony answered.

"I agree and now that we have the tests, we're bound to get better grades going forward."

"I tell you what," Tony solemnly replied. "If my grade doesn't come up, I'm calling a Civil Rights organization."

Tony and Cameron laughed.

Cameron walked side by side with Tony to the next class. At least they were at somewhat more of an advantage now they had the old tests from previous classes. In just a few short months, she would receive her MBA. It gave her a renewed since of hope and confidence to improve her grade.

Chapter 21 when a man loves

Michael stood outside the tall brick building. The facility had to be at least ten stories tall. There were two places Michael disliked the most, jails and hospitals. However, his concern for Tomiko drew him to both places over the past few weeks. He had only been to the jail one other time in his life, when his father decided to discipline his mom for placing ketchup in the refrigerator. Michael remembered intervening on his mom's behalf during a similar event. His father often fell into fits of rage and hit his mom before for burning a piece of toast. His father had an unfair advantage over his mom; he stood six-feet-two inches tall compared to his mom at five-feet-two. He could no longer tolerate feeling helpless and decided the next time his father put his hands on his mother he would have to answer to him. However, Michael ended up blacking out that night when his father hit him. After that, Michael began to work out every day, vowing he would be strong enough to beat his father and protect the woman he loved the most at that time, his mom.

The night his father knocked his mom unconscious a curious neighbor heard the ruckus from her front yard and called the police. They rushed his mom to the hospital and handcuffed his father taking him to jail. His father called him, he was in undergraduate college at that time, to release his property to him and bail him out. Everything in Michael's soul wanted to leave him in jail but his father reminded him of his position in the family.

"I pay for your schooling!" His father fervently exclaimed. "You can leave me in here if you want to but who is going to write a check for your tuition. If I lose business over this, you'll lose your future." That was his father's answer to his questions of why he should come bail him out. James Alexander was a charming man and his life at home was truly personal up until that incident. He built a thriving enterprise as a sports journalist. However, the incident created unwelcomed publicity for the Alexander household. After reports hit the newspapers and sports media outlets, his father publicly announced he and his wife were seeking marriage counseling.

Seeing Tomiko in the hospital put him back in a helpless and vulnerable place. He came here to get answers. Thanks to his friends on the police force, he discovered Charlotte Powell was one of the assailants and she was still in custody. Gregory Simmons bailed out on his own recognizance, which meant he was a first time offender. However, Charlotte was a repeat offender with charges for both violent and drug related crimes.

Michael made his way down the long bland hallway of the county jail. He was definitely in an institutional facility. He would go crazy just looking at the bare walls. The minor inconvenience of visiting the jail was a sacrifice he could make to ensure he protected the woman he loved and Michael had questions he needed answered. Tomiko kept quiet about the incident after she came out of the hospital, but Michael wanted to know why someone would want to harm her.

He walked into a small booth awaiting Charlotte. A woman stood on the other side of the door leading into the inmate's booth area. The booths were sectioned off on the prisoner's side but the stools on the visitor's side didn't have walls or private entry. Michael could only see the top of her wavy hair before the doors opened. When she entered the booth, to his surprise, Charlotte was a decent looking woman. Charlotte sat down, put the receiver hanging on the wall to her ear and initiated the conversation.

"Who are you s'posed to be, my public defender or something?" Charlotte rolled her eyes avoiding eye contact.

"No, I'm not your attorney."

"Well, I ain't got nothing else to say. I told the other Dick all I have to say so until I talk to an attorney and get a bond outta here, ya'll can kiss my ass."

"Charlotte, I'm not a cop either. I'm a friend of-" Michael paused. Charlotte wasn't the friendliest person he ever encountered but what should he have expected. "I'm a friend of Tomiko's. I'm her fiancé."

"Ha!" Charlotte mocked laughter in disbelief. "No this bitch didn't send her fiancé up here." Charlotte's demeanor immediately changed from laughter to anger. "What the fuck do you want?"

"Tomiko didn't send me here. She doesn't even know I'm here. From what I've been told, the two of you used to be really good friends."

"Well you look like the cops to me and like I said I'm not talking."

"Charlotte, I'm not the cops. I'm Michael, Tomiko never mentioned me to you before?"

Charlotte lowered her eyebrows. "No, she never mentioned your name mark! But then again, there's a lot of things she didn't mention to me."

"Ok, Charlotte, let's start over. I just need to know what Tomiko did to make you come all the way from Illinois to Georgia. I'm about to marry this woman and I need answers."

"Sounds like you got problems that don't concern me buddy." Charlotte thought a minute. "But if you help me maybe I can help you."

"Charlotte, I didn't come here for negotiations."

"Well then, I guess this conversation is over. You'll never know the bitch you're marrying."

Michael sat silently. How could he really trust the woman on the other side of the glass window? "You know what, you're right. I shouldn't have come down here. I'm gone."

Michael got out of his chair and hung up the phone when Charlotte motioned for him to sit back down. "I need you to do me a favor. I'll tell you whatever you want, just help me get outta here."

"Why would I help you get out of here?"

"You think Tomiko is some kind of angel and I'm just so crazy that I'd drive all the way down her to beat a bitch's ass I ran with from elementary school. Come on, your tie can't be that tight." Charlotte made fun of his attire. "I don't have any regrets or secrets but, Tomiko, she got a closet full of skeletons you don't even want to know about."

"Really?" Michael listened to Charlotte with reservations.

"You can help me get outta here?"

"Keep talking and we'll see."

"Tomiko and I used to do a lot of things for money when we were younger. Some shit that could've got us killed or hurt in a bad way. It was her idea for us to start tricking when we were sixteen. We both wanted money so we started charging guys to have sex with us, if they were our boyfriends we would just ask them for money to get our hair and nails done or take us shopping. We were such cheap hoes."

Charlotte distantly stared out the glass through the corners of her eyes and shook her head in disappointment.

She looked back towards Michael, "Well, turns out she had a free client that she didn't tell me about. He was my boyfriend then and he is my fiancé now. Tomiko's been sleeping with him for the past eight years and he just told me the other night. I was mad as hell. After I took all the anger I could out on him, I hopped in my car and headed straight to Atlanta to finish my business. So, Mr. Michael, tell me, would you have done anything different?"

"Tomiko has suffered a lot of pain at your hands. I'm not sure if what you are telling me is true but I do know one thing, ruining someone else's life doesn't make yours any better."

"Yeah, well there are two things I don't play about, that's my family and my money. So, don't judge me."

"I'm not here to judge you. Do you have anything else you want to tell me?"

"Michael, I like you." Charlotte smiled. "You seem to be a real classy fellow. I see why Tomiko picked you, but if I were you, I would get as far away from Tomiko as I could. She's toxic. She's a natural liar and you know what they say?"

"What is it *they* say?"

"You can't turn a hoe into a house wife."

"Thanks for your time." Michael ended the conversation abruptly.

"Remember, you promised me you would help me get outta here."

Michael hung up the phone, leaving Charlotte with the phone to her ear. He couldn't hear her voice but her facial expressions let Michael know she wasn't calling him a saint. The only thing he had from that conversation was more questions. Tomiko's silent break was over.

Tomiko lounged on the couch waiting for Michael to return home. Michael suggested that she stay with him, just until she completely healed and felt safe enough to return home.

She tormented herself with a way to tell Michael all the details of her dealings with Charlotte. The veil of lies that covered her true past made it hard for Tomiko to sleep comfortably in his home. She would wake up in the middle of the night sometimes to tell him, but found herself lying right back down.

She made up her mind that today would be the day. There would be no secrets between the two of them and she was going to start by airing her own dirty laundry. Tomiko heard keys and the doorknob turning on the other side of the door. She leaped to her feet anticipating Michael's entrance through the front door. Michael huffed past her without acknowledging her presence and made his way to the bar. He poured himself a glass of vodka on the rocks. Tomiko was immediately worried. Michael never came home and poured a drink that strong unless he had a stressful day. Even on his stressful days, he stopped to kiss her on the forehead before he headed to the bar.

"Honey, what's wrong?" Tomiko asked in concern.

Michael didn't answer. He glanced up at Tomiko without saying a word. He continued to drink down his vodka and then poured another glass. She watched him guzzle the second glass. She raised her eyebrow, "Michael, what's bothering you?"

Michael put his glass down and picked up his briefcase. He headed towards the kitchen island where he opened the case.

"I went to the police station to get a copy of your incident report." He continued to sort through his papers and pulled out a manila folder. "Then, I paid a visit to one of your old friends, Charlotte Powell."

Tomiko's mouth dropped. "Really? Well, what did she say?"

"We're going to play this game Tomiko? Isn't it time that we stop playing games and just start being honest with one another?" He slammed the folder on the counter. "What the hell do you think she said?" Michael placed both hands on his waist and stood authoritatively over her.

She knew she had to clarify things and quickly or the conversation would turn into a verbal brawl and she did not have the strength to fight today. "Michael, I can explain."

"Oh, there's no need to explain now. Charlotte told me all about it. See, you and let me see, what's his name?" He glanced down at his open folder. "Devin, does that name ring a bell? You and Devin have been having an affair. How could I be so stupid?" Michael held his head up and bit his bottom lip to restrain himself from acting irrationally. "I can't believe I trusted you."

"No, that is not what happened Michael."

"Well help me understand!"Michael adamantly exclaimed.

"Michael, please calm down. I can't talk to you when you're upset like this-"

Michael continued, "I mean it all makes perfect sense now. You weren't having sex with me, so I guess this is what you do. I mean-was it worth it?"

"Michael, don't do this."

"Don't do what Tomiko? I figure I can't do any worse than you."

"At least hear my side of the story before you go jumping to conclusions."

"You had ample time to give me your version of the story. I've been waiting to hear your version of the story for weeks now." Michael walked towards Tomiko and placed his hands on the edge of the couch. In an agitated and angry tone Michael murmured, "I've been waiting months to hear your version of the story but you know what, now what you have to say doesn't even matter. You've lied to me, deceived me, and disgraced me. How do you think it makes me feel to find out this from a people that I don't even know?" He shook his head in disbelief. "You know, I sat across from that woman and didn't know if I should believe her or not. Listening to her describe you, it was like she was talking about a completely different person."

Tomiko reached for him but he pulled away. "But Michael, I am a completely different person. You have to believe me." Tomiko restrained her tears.

Tomiko thumbed through the papers. The top page had her company's letterhead, with her name and social security number across the top. "These are my personnel files. Michael, how did you get these? This is confidential."

Michael turned to her in amazement. The only thing she could think of at a time like this was the legality of him possessing her personnel file. "You never cease to amaze me Tomiko."

"Michael, okay, do you want to know the truth or are you going to continue this ranting and raving?" She stood face to face with him. "I know that things seem a bit odd and I know that I have kept a lot from you, but please believe me. The only reason I didn't tell you was because I was afraid."

"Afraid of what Tomiko?"

"Of losing you Michael-I realize how much I truly love you."

"Tomiko, that is such a crop of shit." Michael raised his voice, "If you were afraid to lose me, you should have told me the truth and not let me find out like this."

"I didn't tell you because I was ashamed, and embarrassed, and I didn't want you to think that my past in any way would reflect on our future. But somehow it got all messed up and, baby you have to believe me when I tell you I haven't slept with that men since we've been engaged." Tomiko's eyes filled with tears.

"Tomiko, things are the way they are because you were deceitful. You never told me, even when I asked, why someone would want to do any physical harm to you, other than it was something that happened years ago. I can't sit comfortably knowing that people are out to get you, and I have no clue why."

"Michael, I never meant to deceive you."

"Well that's exactly what you did and you know what else Tomiko? It hurts." Michael began to walk off as Tomiko sat there with nothing left to say. Michael turned to her before he made it completely up the stairs, "The wedding is *off*, and I want you out of my house tonight."

Tomiko already knew there would be no wedding. Michael didn't have to make any formal announcement to her. Michael had been so loyal to her, and she repeatedly caused him pain. It was a rare moment that Tomiko introspectively evaluated her part in conflict. However, in just a few short months, Charlotte accomplished exactly what she set out to do: kill, steal, and destroy, just like a jezebel. She killed Tomiko's spirit, stole her future, and destroyed her relationship.

"Michael, just listen to me and let me explain."

"Don't explain anything to me. Just go now Tomiko!"

"I've been trying to tell you for the longest time. I just didn't know how." She cried out.

"Well, you can thank Charlotte for doing your

dirty work."

Tomiko tried one more waning attempt to convince Michael not to end the relationship. "Please, don't this to me, don't do this to us. I never needed you as much as I need you now. Michael, I love you."

Her pleas fell upon deaf ears. Michael wanted Tomiko completely out of his sight and his life. He couldn't believe all the time he had wasted.

He would never know, but he was the only man she allowed herself to love. Michael walked to his bed and tried to drown out the rage in his mind with music. Tomiko packed up all of her belongings as the jazz music blared out of Michael's bedroom. She looked around the space and realized she practically moved into his place.

Tomiko grabbed as much as she could quickly before walking up the stairs to Michael's bedroom. "I'm not going to be able to get everything tonight. I will come back tomorrow and get the rest."

"You can leave the key on the dresser. I'll have the concierge let you in tomorrow." The words were just as harsh as the ones exchanged in the screaming match they had just finished downstairs. She walked to the dresser, hoping Michael would look her way one last time but he wouldn't; she was invisible to him now. The one person that she had grown to love was now gone.

She could understand his pain. She knew there was nothing she could say or do to change her past. Nothing could undo her past decisions and it was much too late for apologies. Michael did not lift one finger to help her. She wanted to take back all the hurt and pain she caused him.

She finally realized what he had been trying to get her to see from the beginning. There was no man out there that would love her unselfishly, the way that he loved her. All her insecurity about commitment and the choices she made trying to run from love had finally caught up with her as she pulled close the door of the condominium on last time. Michael showed her what love truly meant; he was her love prototype. Tomiko lost and discovered love simultaneously. As she embraced the embodiment of love Michael had to offer her, she also learned love's limits.

Chapter 22 never hurt again

LaShaun stood in the bathroom methodically covering her eyes with shadow, applying a subtle bronze mid-tone and a gold color for her highlight, right below the eyebrow and the bottom of her eyelid. She was dressed from head to hip, with only a black bra worn on her upper torso. She inched closer to the bathroom mirror, anchored her feet in bathroom rug while gently leaning her hips into the edge of the counter for balance. She stretched over the sink until she could almost kiss the glass. Slowly, she traced the lining of her lips with a brown lip pencil and topped them with a coat of shimmering bronze lip-gloss, her perfect duo.

Her hair fell softly on her face and in a few minutes, Jason would ring her doorbell. She anticipated the crowded club, a live concert performance by Young-T and enjoying a night out with Jason again. Jason was setting a good pace for them this year. This would be the second outing in two months.

The doorbell rang as she fastened the last button

on her blouse. She tucked her shirt in the waist of her pants as she walked to the door and peeked at the clock hanging over the television in the living room. Jason arrived promptly at nine o'clock. LaShaun greeted Jason with a smile; he walked in the apartment in an unexpected haste.

"What's up, you ready?" Jason peeked into the living room.

"Well *hello* to you too." LaShaun addressed him snidely.

"Oh, I'm sorry." Jason gave her a hug and quickly kissed her on the cheek. "Hi LaShaun how are you?" He continued looking around the apartment.

"What are you looking for?"

"Nothing, where's Cameron?"

"Are you here to take Cameron out or *me*?"

"Girl stop actin' silly. Where's your roommate?"

"She's out being a grown woman."

"Really, she finally gon' get her some? What's up with her and that boy anyway?"

"Why must you be in everyone else's business?"

Jason laughed and walked back towards the door. "I'm concerned about her. You know Cameron's my girl."

"No, you're just nosy." LaShaun shook her head, still unable to grasp how meddlesome he behaved at times.

"Come on girl, let's get out of here." Jason grabbed LaShaun around her waist and led her towards the door.

"Give me just one second." She twirled out of his arms and rushed back to her bedroom to retrieve her purse and coat.

Jason called to her from the stairway outside her door, "Girl, is that molasses in your booty? You better come on here." Jason called out to her.

"Shut up! I'm coming." LaShaun yelled back

heading to the door.

The line for Club Platinum stretched at least a half a block. Platinum always drew a huge crowd on Saturday nights but with Young-T headlining a show there tonight, the club would soon reach maximum capacity.

"Jason, you know it's hard to get in this club. I can't believe it's only nine thirty and the line is already so long."

"These are the cheap folks. They don't want to pay to get in the club so there here early. Plus the owners hold up the lines as an advertisement strategy."

"Jason, we're here early." LaShaun pointed out to him.

"I know but that's because I wanted to get in before they start turning people away, not because I'm cheap."

"Are you sure it isn't a little bit of both. "LaShaun chuckled.

"Ha-ha-ha," Jason sarcastically laughed. "I'm just sayin', when the club starts filling up they won't let the performers inside if it violates the fire code. I've seen it happen before."

Jason led her to the back entrance of the club and up the stairs where two bouncers sat with their arms folded until they recognized Jason. They both immediately dropped their hands and gave Jason this handshake LaShaun recognized. It was one she saw her brothers and fathers do but somehow just seemed universal among the men she knew. First, the two men would slap hands with one another, open palm; next, automatically, the two men would embrace each other with the free hand and place the fist and forearms of interlocked hands between them.

After the brief exchange between the men, Jason grabbed LaShaun's hand as they continued to make their way into the door and redeemed their tickets for wristbands with the letters V.I.P. on them. LaShaun could get used to the star-studded treatment. She loved V.I.P. access.

Jason led her to the area of the club with red velvet ropes surrounding it. She searched the club for Reese; hoping her friend, the promoter, had legitimate connections. LaShaun could tell it was going to be a long night by the way a couple of females greeted her with cold stare downs. She figured the regular groupies did not need LaShaun competing with them for the men that often hung out in the V.I.P. section, readily spending their cash. Little did they know she already had a man with money and power, a *baller*.

The music blared loud enough that LaShaun could have worn earplugs and still identified the beat and lyrics to the songs the disc jockey played.

"What do you want to drink?" Jason turned to ask LaShaun as they approached the bar.

"Huh?" LaShaun shouted back.

Jason mimed drinking a cup with his hands, "Drink!" he yelled.

"Oh, I'll take a strawberry daiquiri."

"Shaun, this isn't Fat Tuesday's," he yelled in her ear. "They don't sell frozen drinks. Why don't you get a real drink?"

"Well get me whatever." Right when she turned away from Jason, she felt someone bump against her. It would indeed be a long night if this continued to happen.

"Excuse you." LaShaun yelled at the woman.

Reese turned around and laughed at LaShaun's reproach to someone she suspected was a stranger. "Girl, we have to stop bumping into each other like this."

"You were about to get told off in here." LaShaun warned Reese, "don't play with me like that, you know I don't play."

"You are on a date." She motioned to Jason who

was still trying to get the bartender's attention.

"I don't care what I am on and who I am with. Shit, he had better be down. " LaShaun teased her friend. "I see your boy turned out to be somebody, you're here."

"Child please, I am not here with him. I am here with one of the radio show producers who *really* promoted the event. Plus, I have personal reasons for being here tonight." Reese refocused the conversation back on LaShaun, "and you look good! That's the coat you brought when we went shopping?"

"Yes ma'am." LaShaun posed for Reese as Jason finally made it back from the bar with two drinks in his hand.

"Here," He handed LaShaun a tall glass with a murky pink liquid. "They don't have strawberry daiquiris"

"What's this?"

"Sex on the beach, it's just as fruity and nasty." Jason sipped his double shot of whiskey.

"What's up Mr. Jason?" Reese smirked at him.

"Hey Reese, how are you?" Jason smiled flirtatiously.

"I'm just fine. I see you got my girl out of the house."

"Yeah, well you know." Jason gloated.

She turned back to LaShaun. "Well, I will holla at you later. I told my date I was going to the bathroom but I am really trying to look around to see what I can see. Let me get back to this table. I'll talk to you later."

"Bye girl. I'll call you." LaShaun waved as Reese walked off into the sea of people.

"Jay," a hip and well-dressed young man yelled over the loud music to get Jason's attention. His face was charming and boyish. "What's up playa?"

"It ain't nothin'," Jason slapped Calvin's hand and the two gently bumped shoulders. "What it do man?"

"I'm glad you made it out, come sit with us at the booth over here."

Calvin glanced in LaShaun's direction. "Hey beautiful lady," he smiled and extended his hand to introduce himself to LaShaun. "Calvin."

LaShaun took his hand, "I'm LaShaun; very nice to meet you." She rolled her eyes at Jason; at least Calvin had manners.

Jason interrupted the introductions, "You remember ol' girl I was tellin' you about with the endorsement deal for Young."

"Yeah, Urban Gear, that's what's up! Is this shorty?" He pointed to LaShaun.

"No, her girl is the one with the hook up."

"Yeah, my girl Tomiko is working on the marketing for them." LaShaun joined the conversation.

"Yeah man, I talked to her but we haven't had a chance to hook up yet. Young is with it tho'. Ya'll shoulda brought ol' girl with you. I could've introduced her to Young and we could politic a little bit." Calvin started walking towards the stage, "And Jay don't buy any more damn drinks at the bar. That's lame."

"Oh, I was just waiting on you baller-baller."

Calvin laughed with Jason and led them to the other side of the club to a section where another brawly bouncer stood near more velvet ropes. Calvin turned around and pointed to LaShaun and Jason, "They wid me." He patted Jason on his chest with his back palm and the bouncer nodded the two of them into the secured and restricted area.

The area was crowded, filled with Young-T's entourage and at least three women, in every shade and nationality, to each guy. The scent of cologne and cannabis filled her nostrils. The women wore scantily fitted clothing that revealed most of their skin. They grinned and flirted with Young-T's associates to get closer to him. One managed to get an introduction, and sat down next to him. She exuded the happiness of million-dollar lottery ticket winner.

"Young, you remember Jay?" Calvin walked up to the entertainer, Young-T; he wore a thin plaid shirt, a white thermo shirt and slim fit jeans.

"Old fumble the ball when I pass it to him Jay. Of course I remember him." Young-T stood to his feet and greeted him with the 'universal' handshake.

"Man, why you gotta bring up old high school shit?" Jason grimaced.

Jason, Young-T and Calvin went to high school together and played football. Young-T, or Troy, was the quarterback, Calvin and Jason played wide receiver. Jason was the only one on the team to go to college on a scholarship but injured himself in his sophomore year.

"It's just good to see you man. V-dubb told me you'd be here," Troy continued; V-dubb was Calvin's nickname, "Oh, and good lookin' out with the Urban Gear endorsement. I think we're going to meet up with the lady at that firm soon. It sounds real good."

LaShaun smiled and didn't say much while Jason talked with his friends. It gave her comfort to know she played an integral role in the business deal they referenced. She explored the area and found a seat in the midst of the crowded space. She noticed Reese walk into the section with her radio disc jockey date. Reese was much taller than he was and they appeared to be the odd couple at the party. LaShaun began to raise her hand to get her friend's attention by waving Reese towards her but Calvin grabbed her before she made it all the way to the back.

Calvin exchanged a few words with the radio disc jockey. The vertically challenged man raised his hands in retreat and backed away from Reese. Reese and Calvin made their way out of the area and LaShaun realized Jason's friend Calvin was Reese's mainstay for a little while. Reese never mentioned Calvin was Troy's manager or Jason's friend. The night was turning into a soap opera and LaShaun had a front row seat.

Jason walked over to LaShaun and handed her a glass of champagne. "Are you okay?"

"I'm good." LaShaun sat enjoying the music and looked at Jason with a knowing grin. "How come you didn't tell me Reese was dating *your* friend Calvin?"

He shrugged his shoulders, "She didn't want me to tell you."

"But I don't understand why?" LaShaun continued shouting over the music.

"She said something like she didn't want it to change your relationship."

"That's why you guys are always talking and snickering. You make me sick."

"Hey," Jason placed his hand over his chest in the same motion as someone taking an oath, "it wasn't my idea. Are you sure you're good?" He asked changing the topic.

"I'm cool," LaShaun pierced her lips together and sipped her champagne.

"Good, holla at me if you need me."

LaShaun nodded her head up and down as she finished her sip of champagne. Jason went over and talked with Troy and the others until it was time for the live performance. The beat for Troy's new song played loudly as he made his way to the stage. Everyone on the dance floor rushed the stage. Hands waved in the air and the entire crowd repeated the chorus in unison:

"We ride cuz we fly, we ride cuz we live, we ride cuz when we ride you know we ride high, throw your hands in the air if you ride, hands everywhere when you ride."

Jason and LaShaun left the club at about two o'clock. Jason helped LaShaun in the car and got in on the driver side.

LaShaun noticed his gaze, "What are you staring at?"

"You coming to my place or am I staying at your place?"

"We can go to your place." LaShaun insisted, "I don't want to wake Cameron up." She smiled at him sinisterly.

"Don't you have to work in the morning?"

"Just bring me home early."

LaShaun and Jason pulled up to his driveway; she noticed a woman walking from the side of his house with a child on her hip. The women looked, petite and frail. She held the infant bundled in a coat. It was after two in the morning, what crazy woman would have her child out of the house? Jason began slowing down.

"Aw shit!"

"Jason do you know that woman?"

Jason just stared at LaShaun. This was a nightmare come true for him. The woman came yelling down the driveway. "Jason you ain't shit. How dare you go out with some other bitch? Get your ass out of the car Jason right now! Oh, bitch you too!" She pointed to LaShaun.

LaShaun turned to Jason, "At this point, I don't care who she is; she has one more time to call me out my name."

Jason immediately jumped out of his car and left it running as he ran up to the woman; he snatched her by the arm, reached for the child and he held the baby close to his chest.

"Tiffany, why are you out here with the baby like this!"

"Because I know you Jason; I knew you were nothing but a two timing punk ass nigga. That's why I came out here, to see for myself. If you ever want to see your son again you had better send that bitch home and not in your car. I am not playing. Send her home."

The last word queued LaShaun out of the truck. She walked towards the front of the vehicle as shouts came to a cease while she made her way towards the couple. "You got one more time to call me a bitch. I don't care who you are or what the hell you got going on with him. You can refrain from calling me out of my name."

"*Bitch*, I don't know you!" Tiffany rolled her eyes at LaShaun.

LaShaun walked towards Tiffany when Jason handed the baby back to her. Jason rushed to LaShaun and restrained her.

LaShaun hollered over his shoulders, "And that's my point, you don't know me and I don't know you. So holla at yo' boy and leave me out of it."

LaShaun pushed Jason off her, "*Let me go!*" She scurried to the driver side of the truck.

"Where are you going?" Jason asked as she slammed the doors of the truck.

"Oh hell no," Tiffany hollered out. "You betta not let her drive off in your car."

"Tiffany, shut the hell up!" Jason turned back to her. "I got this."

LaShaun eased out of the driveway and Jason began to hit the driver side window while holding on to the car handle. "LaShaun, open the door now. Stop playin'."

LaShaun threw up her two fingers in a peace sign and put her index finger down as she continued to roll back; before she knew it, she fully pulled out the driveway and down the road. She had no idea where she was going, but she had new information to process. She knew where Jason had been spending his time now. Jason had a son and a baby mama. She suspected something was pulling him away from her but she never imagined she would be sitting in Jason's driveway confronted by a raging woman with a baby. She pulled her cell phone out of her purse and called Cameron.

"Hello," Cameron answered the phone.

"*Can you believe this asshole has a baby?*" LaShaun yelled through the phone.

"*Who? Jason?*" Cameron asked not prepared for the news her friend was now sharing with her over the phone.

"Yes, *Jason!* Mr. Golden Boy himself. I'm so pissed off right now. I could kill him."

"LaShaun, calm down and let me meet you somewhere."

LaShaun cried out loudly, "I just don't know how this could happen."

"LaShaun, you shouldn't be driving right now. Pull over somewhere and let me meet you."

"Where are you?"

"Uhm," Cameron answered with reservations, "I'm over Corey's right now but I can leave here and meet you."

"Don't tell Corey anything." All she needed was this to get back to Andre and she was not in the mood to explain anything to Corey or Andre.

"I'm not, where are you?"

"I'm in college park, not far from you."

"Good, I'll see you in a minute."

LaShaun pulled into a nearby gas station, with no patrons and two fill pumps. One of the fill pump signs read full-service, where the gas station attendant would actually pump the gas for customers. She hadn't seen a full-service station in years and it reminded her that she was in the midst of a remote and dark area in College Park; what she and her friends often referred to as the boonies. She sat in Jason's car wishing she had a knife or another sharp object she could use to tear at the seats but nothing was in eyesight of the immaculate vehicle.

Cameron pulled up next to the truck and LaShaun slowly opened the driver door. LaShaun looked at Cameron and before she could say anything, tears began dripping from her eyes.

Cameron hugged her and comforted her, "It's alright. Come on, get in the car."

Cameron dialed Jason's number once LaShaun was in the car and barely allowed Jason to greet her. "You need to come get your car or we're going to give it to the next available dope fiend that walks by; you got ten minutes."

Cameron hung up the phone and sat in the car with LaShaun. LaShaun cried uncontrollably. "I can't believe it, how could he not tell me. At least if he told me I could've made the decision to keep seeing him or not. But he didn't even tell me."

"LaShaun, what do you expect from him? He's an a-hole."

LaShaun laughed because Cameron didn't curse, "An a-hole, you got that right."

"He doesn't deserve you and you already know that."

"I'm just so mad, I can't even blame him. I shouldn't have been so gullible."

"We live and learn."

LaShaun sat in silence staring at the neon lights affixed in the gas station windows advertising the name brand beers carried in the store and an open sign.

Jason pulled up in a car LaShaun had never seen before; based on the pink sunglasses hanging over the rearview mirror, she assumed it was Tiffany's car.

"Oh great, how did he know we were here?" She looked at Cameron as if she were a traitor. "You *called* him?"

Cameron defended herself, "I told him to come get his car or we'd be giving it to the next dope fiend that walked by."

LaShaun folded her arms, "We could've just left it here and let him find it. I'm sure he has some car retrieval device on it or something."

Jason grabbed the passenger door handle of Cameron's car and it didn't budge. "Can you unlock the door please?" He pleaded with LaShaun.

"Can you kiss *my ass* please?" LaShaun sharply answered.

"I would if you'd just unlock the door."

LaShaun looked at Cameron, "I really want to rip his eyeballs out right now."

"Just see what he has to say."

"You're too damn nice. I wish Tomiko was here."

"Oh no, because then I'd be bailing the two of you out of jail. Go ahead and see what he has to say. This should be good."

LaShaun rolled her eyes and unlocked the door. She got out the car and started walking towards Jason's truck. The crisp winter air made the tears cold against her face. She wiped them quickly hoping Jason wouldn't see any sign of her crying.

Jason was unsure how to start the conversation, "After you left, I finally got Tiffany, to calm down."

"That's what you have to tell me? I don't give a damn about Tiffany or you right now."

"LaShaun, I met Tiffany a little before I started dating you. When she told me she was pregnant with Cody, I contemplated proposing to her and letting you know what was going on. I just wanted to be a father to my child and do things the right way." He unlocked his car door and offered LaShaun a seat inside out of the cold. "You want to sit down?"

"I'm good," LaShaun declined his offer. "How old is he?"

"Six months." Jason bowed his head down in shame and began nervously rubbing his head. He thought he had everything under control.

"You have a six month old son. Why didn't you tell me?"

Jason didn't answer her.

"Damn it Jason, why didn't you tell me? You should've let me decide if I would continue seeing you not make the choice for me. It's selfish and wrong Jason!" LaShaun yelled.

"At the time I thought it was best you didn't know. I don't know why I didn't tell you." It was all he could think to say.

LaShaun looked at him while he sat in silence. "Where's your girlfriend now? She let you back out the house?"

"She's not my girlfriend."

"Lucky for her."

"Shaun, I wish this didn't happen like this. At least give me a chance to explain everything. If not tonight, let me come by tomorrow."

"Oh, I'm sorry, so let me see if I got this straight; you're going to sleep with her tonight and see me tomorrow?"

LaShaun waited for his answer but he didn't say anything. "I've seen and heard enough." She walked back to Cameron's car, and pulled the passenger door open. The very sight of Jason incited hateful emotions inside of her. She wished that she had a match she could light so she could watch him blow up while she drove off. She turned to him before she got in the car, "Don't bother calling me, because I won't be available."

He ran to Cameron's side of the car. "Cameron, I never meant for this to happen. Talk to your girl for me. Tell her to forgive me."

"Jason, I gotta leave that between you and her."

He looked back at LaShaun one last time and she rolled her eyes at him and looked out the window. LaShaun shook her head; she restrained her tears with the final thought, *how could I have been such a fool?*

Chapter 23 believe what he says

"Come in and step inside my room
I wanna spend the night with you
Tell me girl would that be cool
I'm not tryna to run no game on you."

Cameron smiled at Corey as she finished the lyrics she composed over the instrumental he produced.

"Let me see that." Corey grabbed the paper from Cameron's hands and smiled. "I'll make you cream in pure ecstasy. I'm not singin' that." Corey laughed as he read the remaining lyrics of the song and put the sheet on his keyboard.

"What's wrong with it?" Cameron asked.

Corey shook his head, "We'll work on the lyrics." He tried to encourage her. "It's a good start. We just gotta put a little more of me in it. I don't say cream."

"Well, what about the first part? Does that sound good?" Cameron asked, attempting to regain some confidence in her lyrical skills.

"Yeah, it's cool." Corey grabbed her wrist and

pulled her closer to him. "It's cool ma'." He kissed her.

"Get off me." Cameron pushed him away, disappointed he did not find her lyrics song worthy.

"Aw, why it gotta be like that?" Corey stepped back from her and sat down on the keyboard stool. "Why don't you have a boyfriend?"

"You want me to have a boyfriend?" Cameron asked sarcastically.

"I don't know why you like me." Corey picked up a bottle of Corona from the side of the keyboard stand and sipped it. "You don't need to be around a man like me. I'm no good for you."

"Corey, what are you talking about?"

"You know why I didn't call you back?" Corey raised his eyebrows.

Cameron didn't know what to say to him. After spending a few evenings with him and growing closer, he withdrew from her without a warning last summer. It was the reason his name became taboo amongst her and her friends. She hoped their relationship would flourish. She never experienced the type of chemistry with others that she felt with Corey and she sometimes wondered if he felt the same way.

"I didn't call you because I knew that I would really like you, and I do. But I couldn't like you like that."

"Okay," Cameron rolled her eyes. "I don't understand. You don't want to like me like what?"

"I would have wanted to make you my girl, and I couldn't do you like that."

"Uh-huh," Cameron still did not understand what Corey was trying to say. They were enjoying each other now and that is all that mattered to her; she lived in the moments they created.

"Never mind, let's go upstairs and watch a movie." Corey turned off his equalizer and recorder. He kept his beer in one hand and grabbed Cameron's hand to lead her upstairs.

Cameron followed Corey with hesitation. She let the words play back in her head. 'I knew that I would want to make you my girl.' It all seemed reasonable to her.

"What movie do you wanna watch?" Corey walked to the DVD stand next to his 52' inch widescreen television.

"I don't know; you pick." Cameron called to him as she walked to the kitchen. "Do you want something out of here?"

"Yeah, bring me another beer."

"You don't need another beer." Every time she came over, Corey had some type of alcoholic beverage in his hand. She worried about his health — mental and physical.

"I'm doing better. I would usually have a bottle of Hennessey by now. I downgraded to beer." Corey laughed and walked into the kitchen behind Cameron.

The doorbell rang before he made it into the kitchen. "Grab me a beer ma'." He pleaded with her before heading towards the front door.

Cameron looked back at him, unimpressed that his downgrade from cognac to beer was a major feat for him.

Cameron could hear P-Body at the door. She walked to the refrigerator to take out the water jug.

Corey called to her, "Hey, I'm running to the store. Do you need anything while I'm out?"

"No, I'm good." Cameron called back to him.

Corey ran in the kitchen and gave her a kiss. "I'll be right back. You sure you okay?"

"Yeah," she smiled.

Corey jogged out the kitchen. "Be right back. Don't go anywhere." He turned around and pointed to her while backing out the kitchen.

"I won't." Cameron smiled. Her spirits lifted at

the thought of her and Corey actually being an item. She enjoyed his company. It made her feel young again. She thought about the partnerships they could create. He could produce and she could write the songs. They could be a modern day Peaches and Herb, Sonny and Cher, Beyoncé and Jay-Z. Their combined talent and synergy could put them at the top in the music industry.

Cameron poured her water in a glass and leaned on the counter daydreaming of them as a power couple, Corey and Cameron in bright lights, sold out concerts, records topping the charts. She smiled to herself and walked towards the table. She sat down and noticed an empty dark green Remy Martin bottle next to a vase of half-dead roses. A card accompanied the ensemble. How could she miss a bouquet of half-dead roses sitting on the table next to a bottle of Remy Martin and a card?

Cameron picked up the card next to the empty bottle of Remy, and read the greeting line, 'To the Man I Love.'

Cameron paced back and forth in the kitchen before deciding what to do. Should she leave or stay to confront him? The one thing she had to remember, when a man tells a woman who he is she had better listen. He was right about one thing; she did not need to be with a man like him.

Cameron walked downstairs to the basement and grabbed her keys off the couch. She ran back up the stairs and grabbed her coat out of the closet. If she moved quickly, she could be out before Corey got home.

Only a fool would listen to all that gibberish Corey spit in her ear tonight. 'I would have really liked you.' He had no idea how close she was to losing her virginity. It did not take much, just some decency and honesty. She just needed him to meet her halfway. In between those lines he could have dropped in a 'I can't be with you 'cause I got a girlfriend.' That would have made things clearer to her.

Cameron hurried towards the door.

"Hey where are you going?" Corey asked as she nearly bumped into him on the way out.

"I have to go." Cameron attempted to keep her response vague and avoid confrontation.

"You comin' back?"

"Corey," Cameron paused trying to build up the courage to accept the truth, "do you have a girlfriend?"

"*What*?"

"*Girl-friend*?" Cameron reiterated. "The card and flowers on the table, are they from your girlfriend?"

"That's nothing that you have to worry about."

"Why is that?"

"You and I aren't in any committed type of relationship."

"So, you can kiss on me and lead me on as long as we're not in any kind of committed relationship but you don't have to tell me if you're seeing someone else."

"I'm just not obligated to explain that to you. You feel me."

"Well, if you have a girlfriend I can't continue to see you."

"Do what you gotta do ma'."

Cameron put on her coat and walked out the door. She tried to hold back the tears, but they trickled down one at a time. What kind of man would paint such a picture of their future together, only to let her down so harshly? Surely, this is not how soul mates treated one another. Then again, Corey drowned his soul in eighty-proof liquor. He could not decipher his soul from the spirits that he allowed to enter his body day after day.

Cameron knew firsthand the effects of alcoholism on families. She would never knowingly subject herself to it. Especially, after growing up with the painful memories of the fights her parents would have because her mom would become disgracefully drunk. She would arrive late to school with her hair half braided because her mom was too drunk to finish it the night before and too hung over to finish it that morning. Embarrassment was the only childhood memory she could think about when reminiscing on her mom's alcohol bouts. She wanted desperately for Corey to be the one for her but she had to protect herself from disappointment.

Chapter 24 worthy of love

Tomiko stood in the boardroom as Young-T and his entourage filled the chairs surrounding the mahogany elongated table. Chad sat to the right of Tomiko with heightened anticipation.

Tomiko extended her hand to greet Troy and Calvin. "Hello Calvin," she nodded towards Troy, "Troy, it's so nice to finally meet you in person. Please let me introduce you to Chad McIntyre, he's the CEO of Urban Gear."

Chad stood to his feet and greeted both men with a handshake.

"I will briefly explain why we are all here today. Although we've had some preliminary discussions with both parties, I wanted to bring you together to talk about how we can create synergy around the Urban Gear and Young-T brands. I feel like this collaboration will be very profitable for both of you and this is an opportunity for you all to share the vision for your individual brands." Tomiko smiled at Troy and Chad. "So, with that being said, I'll let Chad tell you a little more about Urban Gear's product line and then we can get down to business."

"Thanks Tomiko," Chad grinned and leaned forward and placed his forearm on the conference table. "Urban Gear, as you are aware, makes some of the most trending fashions in hip-hop culture today. We are looking for a spokesperson to stand behind the brand and promote the men's fashion line. Tomiko put me in contact with you," Chad interjected after a slight pause, "by the way; love your new single brotha."

"Thanks man, 'preciate that," Troy humbly responded.

"So, we thought perhaps Urban Gear would be a product line you could stand behind and endorse to your fan base." Chad handed Troy a portfolio, "here are some of the new designs we have coming out in the fall."

Tomiko interjected as Calvin and Troy viewed the portfolio, "We want to put your face, or brand, with the Urban Gear brand. What that entails is shooting commercials, wearing the brand at public appearances, such as shows and other public events."

"So, I can't wear anything but Urban Gear?" Troy asked alarmed and turned to Calvin. "That's kind of asking a lot. I mean, I like the gear, don't get me wrong, I just don't wanna have to wear it every day."

"Well, we aren't asking you to sport it every waking moment of your life but we are providing you the wardrobe and a pretty hefty endorsement offer." Tomiko responded.

Troy raised his eyebrows, "Fo' real!"

Calvin shook his head in agreement, "And you don't have to exclusively wear the clothing, just when you're at public events like your performances, award shows, interviews, and stuff like that," Calvin turned to Tomiko to make sure he was correct. "Am I right?"

"Yes, and everything will be explicitly laid out in

your contract."

"How much are we talking here?" Troy asked.

"Seventy-five grand for a yearlong contract plus a wardrobe," Chad responded.

Troy looked to Calvin, "What do you think about it? You think it's a go?"

"I say let's look over the contract. Send it to the legal team and let them look through the paperwork."

"We can do that; we can do that today." Tomiko tenaciously responded.

"Yeah," Troy nodded. "I'm feeling this though. It sounds like a good deal."

"I'll get my assistant to send over the contract right after this meeting." Tomiko made a notation in her planner to have David send the documents to Calvin.

They all rose to their feet and in conclusion of the meeting shook hands; including the three men that came along with Troy for what Tomiko assumed to be protection.

"Thanks for your time," Tomiko led them out the boardroom to the elevators. The endorsement deal was closer to being finished and another task off her plate.

Tomiko stared out her window overlooking downtown, wondering how she survived it all. She could only think where she would be if she did not have the encouragement from her friends. Her work atmosphere drastically changed, mostly due to her shift in priorities. The desire to work until her fingers fell off no longer took precedent over enjoying her life. Tomiko reached a point of incompleteness because she relied so heavily on her career to fill her sense of self-worth. Experiencing love with Michael made her realize there was more to life than a successful career.

Tomiko prayed aloud while turning back to her office desk, "Lord, give me strength to make it through."

Praying was something she learned to do from

her grandmother and she used it often when there was nothing left for her to do physically. She fought through bouts of depression in an attempt to forgive herself from her past life. The God she knew would forgive her as long as she no longer continued in her transgressions. If God was the only person to forgive her, then she could forgive herself.

After praying, Tomiko's office door inched open. She looked up from her desk and noticed a male shoe making its way into her office. She stared at the foot, anxiously waiting for the visitor to step into her office. Tomiko aided the process with a preemptive greeting, "How can I help you?"

Michael peered in the door to be sure he was not interrupting her, "Yeah I uhm-I uhm, came to bring you this." Michael handed Tomiko her Bible.

Tomiko was surprised to see him. Three months had passed since she last spoke to him. "I-I must've overlooked while I was packing." Tomiko stumbled over her words. She wanted to make this moment count. "Wow, thanks but you didn't have to bring this all the way up here but I'm glad you're here."

"Yes, I did."

Tomiko looked up at him, surprised by his response. "Michael, I know-I really messed up. I get it. I'm so sorry. I would give anything to make this right again."

"Tomiko let me start by saying I know we've been through a lot in the past few months and to be completely honest with you, I just didn't know how to handle it all. I didn't know what to believe."

Silence fell over the room. Michael had Tomiko's complete attention.

"Tomiko, I love you and there is nothing that can change the way I feel about you; but I can't live with a liar and I can't live with deception. It's not my style, and it's never been."

Tomiko silently choked up as she exhaled deeply; she could not respond to him verbally but everything in her wanted to tell him she was sorry and ready for love.

"You know after you left I thought about all the things that you said, and you know what stood out in my mind the most?"

She shook her head and answered, "No."

Michael stepped towards her and put the side of her face in the palm of his hand, "You told me you loved me and I believe you meant it. You know how I know?" Michael paused again. "Because of all the time we've dated, you've never told me you loved me and I'm not ready to give up on you."

Michael moved Tomiko in ways that she could have never thought possible. She sat there in the presence of his love for her. She thought of how he always stood beside her when times got tough; he was the constant in her life. She was uncertain if he would stay with her after he found out about all the things that haunted her past, but the more he found out the more he was willing to fight. Any flaw she found in her life, she had tried to cover it because she never gave Michael credit for loving her beyond their circumstances.

"Tomiko, I want us to start all over again. If that's okay with you?

"Yes. I would love to start over again with you."

Michael gently kissed her lips in covenant, "No more secrets; no more lies." Michael looked deeply into Tomiko's eyes, "It's about me and you."

Tomiko agreed with a silent nod.

"Lunch at twelve?" Michael asked.

"I wouldn't miss it for the world."

"See you at twelve; I'll be downstairs waiting on you."

"Okay." Standing there in her office, she was a first hand recipient of unconditional love and she learned the extremes people go through for one another when they are in love. Michael was the perfect teacher.

Tomiko felt as if butterflies danced in her stomach. Michael coming to her office was one of the last things she expected. She could not imagine a better make up. She called David to arrange her calendar.

"Yes Ms. Bordeaux?" David answered in expectance.

"David, I'll be out for the rest of the day."

"Should I cancel your staff meeting?"

"Reschedule it for me. Thanks."

Tomiko packed up her belongings and made her way to the main floor lobby. When she arrived on the ground floor of the office building, Michael handed her a bouquet of red roses. She grabbed the roses and placed her arm around his. Together they walked outside the building to what Tomiko felt was a new destiny. She wished she could've learned love's lessons sooner, but there was comfort in knowing she would spend the rest of her life with a man that cared for her and no matter what, she was worthy of love.

Chapter 25 the second time around

LaShaun waited in the patio area of the Friday's in Buckhead on Peachtree Street. The spring weather made it idea for a meal on the patio. LaShaun enjoyed the seventy-degree weather without the humidity, clear skies and a bright sun shining down on her while she sat awaiting Andre. Her top leg rhythmically moved up and down as she tried not to lose any patience. Andre was late. She had already been there for fifteen minutes.

Her large sunglasses helped block the suns bright rays and on days like this, she often times preferred outside seating over the restaurant's frigid air conditioning during the springtime.

As LaShaun turned around to grab her purse from the back of the chair, Andre was waiting directly behind her. She jumped up from her chair before she realized who he was; Andre grabbed her close to him so she could not harm him with a quick elbow.

"It's okay baby; I'm here." Andre smiled with his genuinely warm and beautiful smile. LaShaun remembered how it captivated her the first time they met on Brownsberry's campus.

"Boy, you play too much!" She frowned and pushed him away from her.

"How do you do it?" Andre sucked his teeth and bit his lower lip in an incredulous manner.

LaShaun looked at him in a confused way and an attitude, "Do *what*?"

"Still turn me on after all these years."

LaShaun looked away from him. She was not even buying his pick-up lines. "Boy, I don't have time for this. Are we eating or what?"

"Are you treating?"

"*Fool*, you invited me here. No I'm not treating." She insisted offended.

"I'm just playing with you. Let's find a seat."

"We can sit right here."

Andre sat across from her and stared before he began his quest. "So, where's your man?"

LaShaun busted out in laughter. "Don't even try it."

"What?"

"You ain't slick, trying to pry into my personal life. Where's your girlfriend?"

"I don't have one. So, like I said, who are you seeing?"

"You wouldn't know him if I told you his name."

LaShaun didn't want to answer the question. If she said no one, then Andre would feel like he could just walk right back into her life, plus she did not want to talk to her ex-boyfriend about her ex-lover.

"Okay, well you can answer this; is he treating you right?"

LaShaun sighed deeply. Andre would monopolize on any signs of her unhappiness. She already knew the game, "Dre, what are you getting at?"

"I just want to make sure my girl is happy. You

know just because I couldn't be there to make you happy doesn't mean I wouldn't want to know that someone else is treating you better. Am I so wrong for that?"

LaShaun didn't answer. The waiter was ready to take their order.

"Well, I'll guess that you are either unhappy or not seeing anyone at all because if you were seeing someone that was making you happy, I have a feeling I would be hearing about it."

"You don't know me." LaShaun rolled her eyes and placed her order with the waiter that seemed quite amused by their conversation. "I'm having the chicken quesadillas." LaShaun pointed while handing the waiter the menu. LaShaun thought, what *a relief to be out with someone and order my own food.*

The waiter turned to Andre, "And you sir?"

"Yeah, lemme get these chicken wangs." He pointed to the menu item.

"No problem, I'll be back with your orders."

"So yo' man let you out of the house today." The thought of LaShaun not being with anyone gave Andre some fuel to run on.

"Look, don't start that again. I am a free woman. Man or no man I do what I want to do."

"Oh really, that's funny, I remember when you were my woman, I wouldn't dare let you out my sight looking like that; not by yourself. I may have been crazy but I wasn't stupid."

"Maybe that's why you're not my man." LaShaun teased him.

"Oh you got jokes, huh." Andre became a bit more serious. He came here on a mission. Only he knew what was really going on in his head. He wanted LaShaun back and he was willing to do whatever it took to get her back. "Man, I miss Atlanta."

"Yeah, Atlanta is okay."

"Yeah but I miss you even more."

LaShaun should have known that it was coming. Why would she set herself up to be in this intimate setting with Andre? "Dre, don't start that."

"What? Don't start being honest. I thought that was something you always wanted from me, honesty." He tried to mimic her expression.

"Shut up."

"Well I got even better news. You know I've been here for a week now. Guess what I've been doing?"

"I don't know." LaShaun answered disinterested, "What?"

"I'm looking for a job. I'm moving back to Atlanta next month. Being back here and seeing all my homeboys; seeing you," Andre allowed LaShaun to ponder on his revelation, "shit, it really got me hype about moving."

LaShaun sat quietly, listening to Andre's plans.

"Shaun" He demanded her attention as she stared into a trance at her shoes.

LaShaun raised her head from the spot where she zoned Andre out and looked into his eyes. Andre back in her life permanently would be somewhat of a challenge. She was just reassessing her life without Jason. She never considered how her life may be if Andre moved back to Atlanta.

"Shaun, I need you to know that when I get my stuff together and situated out here, I'm coming to get you and nothing or no one is going to stop me. So tell that punk, there's a new sheriff in town."

LaShaun vaguely smiled as she reminisced about Jason, the baby and the baby mama. She raced back to the day she made up her mind that she and Andre would no longer be together. There was just more going on right now than she really wanted to accept. Andre is moving back, Jason is a father, and she did not want to deal with anything that involved using her emotional energy.

"Andre, if you want to move back here I'm excited and happy for you but please don't move back here thinking things are going to work out between the two of us. I-I'm just not ready to deal with that right now."

"Shaun, I'm not trying to put any pressure on you at all and *I* am definitely moving back. I guess time will tell with you and me. I just thought you should know my intentions."

Andre paused shortly and continued, "I am going to be in town for the next couple of weeks. I'll probably hook up with Corey so maybe you and Cameron can come by and hang out with us?"

LaShaun answered him with a stare to assure him there was no chance she would be playing matchmaker between Cameron and Corey again.

"Even if both of you don't make it, I need to see you again before I leave."

"That might be doable."

After they finished their meals, Andre made his way out of his seat while LaShaun gathered her purse. He reached for her hand to help her up and gave her the number to the place he was staying.

"I'll be over P-Body's, so it's cool to call me over there."

"Oh, how is P-Body?"

"He's straight; he just bought a house in Austell."

"A house, that's good."

They walked out the doors of the restaurant and handed the valet their tickets. The valet drove LaShaun's truck around before Andre's rental car.

Andre pointed to LaShaun as she was getting into her truck, "You better call me, girl."

LaShaun threw on her shades and waved goodbye.

Chapter 26 love will bring him back

Cameron hung her graduation robe and hood on the hook in the back seat of her car. She pulled up her black stockings by the waistband, through her dress one last time. She hated pantyhose; they always seemed to ride down her ample buttocks and she refused to wear larger size pantyhose because they fell around her ankles. In preparation for her trip to the Virgin Islands, Cameron had lost twenty more pounds. She somehow managed to convince LaShaun and Tomiko to join her and her classmates.

Cameron found an inexpensive graduation dress at a discount retailer. It was simple and black. She flattened her dress to her thighs and scooted into her car seat, being careful not to tear a run in her pantyhose. She had to pick up her mom and dad from the downtown hotel they stayed in and be at the school's football field by eight o'clock in the morning.

Cameron and the others managed to band together after getting a hold of Meagan's test results. Meagan became a part of their study group and she was even going on the trip with them Memorial weekend. Cameron reserved rooms in a completely different resort from the others purposely. Although she got along with Meagan, she was not quite ready to be her best friend. The rest of the group really liked Meagan and Cameron realized she might have rushed to judge her. They all ended up passing the Theories of Management course with a B.

When Cameron made it to the hotel, she had her parents called down from their room. She could hear her mother before she saw her.

"I asked you to pack my cigarette box for me. If you do what I ask you to do, we wouldn't have these problems. Now my nerves are all bad Bill! Damn it!"

Cameron began softly beating her head against the steering wheel and whispering to herself, "Why, why, why?" She looked up and hopped out the car to referee. "Mom, dad, can we just get in the car so I'm not late for graduation?"

Katie propped her shoulders back and walked to the passenger side door of Cameron's car. Her husband grabbed the handle and opened the door for her. "Thank you," she looked down at him, trying to keep her composure.

Cameron could tell her mom had already been drinking that morning. After her mom got in the car, her father came around to give her a kiss on her cheek.

"Good morning baby girl!" He smiled and squeezed into the back of her Honda.

"Dad, are you sure you don't want to grab the rental and follow me?" Cameron looked at her dad through the rearview mirror. "Mom can ride with me and you can follow me there. It's really close."

"Naw, baby girl, I'm good." He raised his head

up and bumped the roof. "Maybe I will follow you."

Cameron nodded her head in agreement, "I'll wait for you to pull the car around."

It perplexed Cameron that a loving man like her father could end up with such an ornery woman. Cameron never remembered a time when her mom was sober, although her brother Tey said she wasn't always like that; Cameron truly wished she could have seen the better days.

"Mom, are you alright?"

"Oh baby, I'm fine. Glad to see my baby graduating again!" Her mom turned to look out the window, but Cameron noticed tears rolling down her face.

"Mom, what's wrong?"

Cameron's mom sulked a little and tried to stop more tears from falling. She turned and looked at Cameron, "I'm just so proud of you. I wish I could've been a better mom. I'm so proud of you Cameron. Don't ever forget that. You hear me?"

"Mom, I know." Cameron reached over and hugged her mom, "I love you!"

"I love you too baby." Katie grabbed tissue out of her purse, "Whew! Let's get going so you're not late." She dabbed her face with the tissue making sure not to smear the mascara on her face.

"Yep, dad just pulled up behind us."

They pulled into the parking garage across from the school's football field and Cameron handed the tickets to her mom and dad. "Okay you guys, get a good seat. I have to go line up. I love you!"

Cameron waved and quickly walked to the doors leading into the stadium locker room. There she found all her classmates lined up for the procession. When she walked in, she found a sea of black graduation caps with gold and red tassels and hoods. It was a moment of excitement and frustration. She still hadn't landed a job after graduation. In the procession line, she was not near anyone she knew and of course, she was in the back of the line because of her last name. When she did marry, she hoped her husband's last name started with an A.

Tony walked to the back of the line to speak to her, "Hey Pookie!" He reached in and gave her a hug.

"Hi Tony," Cameron hugged him back. It was such a surreal day for her and she felt they had been on such a long journey together to get out of school. "Are your parents here?" she asked him.

"My mom is; my dad had to stay behind and take care of business. The one he wants me to come work with him on." Tony answered discouraged.

"Well, at least you have a job. Don't complain." Cameron yelled over all the noise from all six hundred other conversations taking place.

"I guess you're right," Tony hollered back, "I'll see you in the islands! I'm going to get back in line, see you after the ceremony." Tony walked off and Cameron leaned on a wall nearby and stepped out of her heels. She had to reserve her foot pain for when it was actually necessary. She reached down to pick up her heels and looked up to see a tall modern young professional in a black tailored suit, white shirt and black tie near her. He smiled at her and for a second, she thought he was an illusion.

"Josh?" She asked in disbelief.

"It's me in the flesh baby!" He opened his arms with a dozen roses in one hand and a card in the other. Cameron walked closer to him and hugged him, smelling his cologne and placing her head firmly in his chest. She missed him more than she could ever let him know. She held on to him for a minute and stopped herself from letting go of the tears that were on the cusps of her eyelids.

"Josh, I can't believe you're here."

Josh held her as long as she held him, "I'm here,

believe it."

Cameron finally stepped back and looked at the flowers and the card. "Are those for me?"

"Actually, no they're not," Josh pulled the flowers closer to him. "They're for someone else."

"Oh, who are you here for?" Cameron wanted to retract her presumptuous remark. How could she just assume Josh was there for her? She did send him an invitation but he had other classmates that could've sent him one too.

"Cameron, of course these are for you. You think I'd fly from D.C. to see anyone else here?"

Cameron's smile lit up her face. "Why would you play like that?" She hit him in his chest.

"It was easy." Josh looked at her, as she smelled the roses. "I missed you Cameron."

Cameron looked at him, wishing she could apologize for being naïve and close minded. The feelings were mutual. "Josh, I missed you too."

"I put a voucher in there for you to come fly and see me anytime you want. I hope you use it."

"Of course I will," She held the roses and the card in one hand and grabbed Josh's hand. "Oh, you gotta meet my parents."

"You don't think it's a little too soon for that?"

Cameron looked at Josh as if she had to explain, she'd forgotten what a joker he was, "Why are you so silly?"

"I don't know, lead the way kamikaze."

Cameron found her parents seated in the stadium and gave her roses to her mom to hold. Tomiko and Michael had found her parents too. Andre and LaShaun were fussing a couple of seats down from them. "Andre, let me sit on this side so I'm closer to Tomiko and Cameron's parents."

"Why can't you just sit there Shaun? I mean you can't be away from Tomiko a minute."

Tomiko interjected, "Uhn-uhn, leave me out of this one Dre."

"You know what just forget it." LaShaun leaned back in her seat, folding her arms.

The stadium seats hadn't filled yet, but the crowd was growing.

Cameron and Tomiko shared a knowing glance with one another. Andre and LaShaun's relationship picked up right where it left off. Cameron didn't know if that was healthy or not but LaShaun seemed content. She turned her attention towards her parents. "Mom, dad, this is Josh."

"*Josh*? Who are you?" Katie exclaimed.

"Mom, Josh is a really good friend. He helped me get through this program."

"Oh, ya'll think I can't see through the charades huh? My baby is dating a *white boy!*" Cameron's mom yelled in laughter.

Josh blushed amused by the comment, "Good morning Mrs. Turner."

"Josh, if you don't mind my wife, you will do just fine." William warned him.

"Mom, do you have to embarrass me every chance you get?" Cameron turned towards Tomiko who chuckled at it all. "Tomiko, what is funny?"

"Your face," Tomiko laughed. "Leave your mom alone; we will make sure Josh is safe. Come on, sit with us."Tomiko insisted.

"I'm really fine." Josh fixed his suit coat and walked down the aisle with Tomiko to a seat nearby.

"Please keep him on the far end," Cameron pleaded with Tomiko.

Cameron's mom looked around, "Is there a bar somewhere near here? Are they serving liquor in this stadium?"

Cameron rolled her eyes, "Mom, *please!*"

"What?" Her mom shouted, "Ok, ok, I'll wait till

lunch."

"Baby girl, go get in line, they'll be starting in a minute." Her dad ushered her out of the aisle.

"Alright, see you guys!" Cameron walked back to her position in the processional.

"Almost too late Ms. Turner," Dean Sutherlin came by to greet everyone in line, dressed in his graduation regalia.

"Hi Dean Sutherlin, I had to escort my guest to his seat. I've been here though."

"Congratulations Ms. Turner," he stuck out his hand and Cameron shook it.

"Thanks!"

Moments later, the processional music started. Cameron held her stomach to calm her nerves. Today marked the beginning of a path she could not have predicted for herself, but she received it with gratitude. There was no way to redo the past, but there was the opportunity to take advantage of every moment going forward.

Chapter 27 to all the men we love

Cameron adjusted her seat on the airplane. She promised Tomiko and LaShaun she would ride in the middle and they could have the aisle and window seats on the plane. She elbowed LaShaun on one side and Tomiko on the other as she tightened her belt. They both looked at her awaiting an apology, but Cameron had done it intentionally.

"What?" Cameron teased them.

"See, you know you are wrong. That's what," Tomiko pointed at her. "That's okay, bartender!"

"Wait, I thought you weren't drinking anymore?"

"Don't worry about me drinking, and why didn't we get first class seats again?" Tomiko asked.

"Because you didn't pay for the upgrades," LaShaun interjected.

Cameron sank into her seat ignoring Tomiko's complaint and question, "I am sure ready for this trip."

"Right? We deserve this, girl," LaShaun agreed. "I'm so glad I let you talk me into going even though I don't have but a couple hundred dollars to my name."

"That's alright, we rolling with a managing partner. She can write this all off as a business expense. She got this!" Cameron jokingly teased Tomiko.

"I'm not losing my job for ya'll." Tomiko retorted with her index finger up waiting for the flight attendant.

"You owe me. Remember?" LaShaun snapped back.

"For what?"

"Jason and Young-T," LaShaun reminded her.

"Ok, this drink is on me." Tomiko replied.

The flight attendant arrived and pressed the overhead attendant light off, bent near Tomiko and smiled, as trained, "What can I get you ladies?"

"I would like three glasses of wine, one chardonnay and two merlots."

"Thanks for not getting me a merlot, yuck!" LaShaun cringed at the thought of tasting wood again.

The attendant arrived shortly after with three plastic wine glasses and three personal bottles of wine.

Tomiko held up her glass after pouring her wine, "A toast…"

"Yes, a toast to me." LaShaun joked.

"No seriously, a toast to us!" Tomiko raised her glass.

"I'll drink to that!" LaShaun put her lips to her glass but Cameron abruptly stopped her from sipping it.

"Wait," Cameron invoked their attention, "this may be the first time in our lives where we have all had men in our lives that we generally care and care about us. Michael is a God send for you Tomiko, and Andre, well the jury is still out on him, but at least you seem happy."

"Wait, what is that supposed to mean? I don't think I like this toast." LaShaun frowned.

"And you finally got some sense and start dating Josh with is fine ass." Tomiko interjected.

"Josh is my friend and we are going to take things slowly. He's so far away so, we just have to see."

Tomiko yawned teasing Cameron, "Boring! I mean, how slow can you go? You have known the man for two years; just gon' get you some already."

"Anyway-" Cameron ignored her and grinned, "I do like having someone that I can call a friend and my man."

"Ladies," Cameron raised her glass up. "This toast, is to all the men we love!"